PANIC IN PITTSBURGH

ROY MacGREGOR

Tundra Books

Published in Canada by Tundra Books, a division of Random House of Canada Limited,
One Toronto Street, Suite 300, Toronto, Ontario M5C 2V6

Published in the United States by Tundra Books of Northern New York,
P.O. Box 1030, Plattsburgh, New York 12901

Library of Congress Control Number: 2012947612

Library and Archives Canada Cataloguing in Publication

MacGregor, Roy, 1948-
       Panic in Pittsburgh / Roy MacGregor.

(Screech Owls)
ISBN 978-1-77049-419-0. – ISBN 978-1-77049-424-4 (EPUB)

        I. Title. II. Series: MacGregor, Roy, 1948- Screech Owls series.

PS8575.G84P36 2013   jC813'.54   C2012-905833-5

We acknowledge the financial support of the Government of Canada through the
Canada Book Fund and that of the Government of Ontario through the Ontario
Media Development Corporation's Ontario Book Initiative. We further acknowledge
the support of the Canada Council for the Arts and the Ontario Arts Council for our
publishing program.

ONTARIO ARTS COUNCIL
CONSEIL DES ARTS DE L'ONTARIO

Designed by Jennifer Lum

www.tundrabooks.com

Printed and bound in the United States of America

1 2 3 4 5 6   18 17 16 15 14 13

For Raphaël Jacques Macgregor Dalle,
France's first Screech Owl.

1

They were laughing at him, and Travis Lindsay knew it, and he knew why. He'd been "*creamed*."

But no way was he going to give them any satisfaction from their stupid little trick. He simply sat there, staring straight ahead, pretending not to notice the snickers. Inside, he was laughing right back at them.

Travis had dozed off almost as soon as their bus pulled out of the airport. There had been a delay before the airplane carrying the Screech Owls took off. Another delay when it landed and they had to wait for a ground crew and a gate. Then there was a long wait for the luggage carousel to start coughing up the team's backpacks and hockey equipment. Travis was tired by the time they got on the highway, and the heat on the bus had been turned up too high.

But now Mr. Dillinger, the Screech Owls' manager, was calling for them all to pay attention. He was standing up near the driver, with two fingers stuck in the sides of his mouth as if they were necessary to hold up his big mustache. He blew sharply – loud as a referee's whistle – and everyone on the bus stopped giggling at Travis.

"Listen up, now!" Mr. D shouted over the roar of the tires. "You are about to see a sight that no one should miss. We're going into the Fort Pitt Tunnel, and what you see when we get to the other side is going to take your breath away. Okay? Everyone ready for a treat?"

"*YES!*" several of the Owls shouted at once.

It was dusk on a cold evening in early January. In the brief moment of darkness after they entered the tunnel before the bus' interior lights came on,

Travis deftly cuffed the top of his head to remove the high "ice cream cone" of shaving cream that some smart aleck – *Nish would be a good guess* – had sprayed on him while he slept. He wouldn't give the others the pleasure of seeing him discover he was walking around with a second head. It was hardly the first time Travis had been "creamed." Sadly, he knew it wouldn't be the last. Not so long as Wayne Nishikawa was a member of the Screech Owls.

Travis would bide his time, and then he'd get even with Nish. He had lost count of the number of times a teammate, never Nish, had woken up to find a mound of shaving cream riding light as air on his or her head. How Nish kept thinking this was funny was beyond Travis. Much about Nish was beyond Travis – and beyond most of the Screech Owls, for that matter.

The long tunnel glowed yellow with lights along the ceiling and wall. There were cars ahead, their rear lights flaring red, and cars behind, their sun-bright headlights running along the wall as the tunnel slowly turned. Up ahead, Travis could see an opening, but nothing beyond it.

"Ready?" Mr. D called out, his big mustache bouncing with anticipated delight.

"READY!"

They shot out of the Fort Pitt Tunnel with night falling, their surroundings suddenly pitch-black after the bright yellow lights of the tunnel they had just come through.

It was snowing lightly, and the headlights of the bus reflected off the large white flakes, surprising and partially blinding those looking through the windshield.

Travis felt as if they were floating on air through the falling snow. It reminded him of "The Magic Carpets of Aladdin" ride at Disney World, a feeling of rising and then falling slowly, effortlessly, silently. And spread out before the Owls through the wide, clear windshield was a city of lights – lights colored blue and red in some of the skyscrapers, lights on the bridges heading over the river, lights from the cars snaking through the streets. It was beautiful.

"Welcome to Pittsburgh!" Mr. D announced, as if he himself had built the city and lit the bridges.

The Screech Owls cheered and shouted out their approval. They were here for the Peewee Winter Classic, the biggest hockey tournament ever to be played on outdoor ice. They would be playing at Heinz Field, home of the Pittsburgh Steelers football club, in front of more than sixty-five thousand seats, if not quite as many fans. But no matter how many empty seats there might be at the final, it was certain that the championship game would be seen by more fans than any peewee hockey game in history.

Nish might finally get into the *Guinness World Records*. Not by mooning the most people in history, or by stuffing more straws into his big yap than anyone had ever done – but as part of a *team*, if the Owls made it to the final.

"*Hey!*" a voice growled from behind Travis.

He didn't need to turn to know who it was.

"*Our boy Travis lost his head!*" Nish squealed.

Everyone laughed but Travis. He stared blankly at Nish – the defenseman's face bright enough to light a dozen Pittsburgh bridges – and shrugged as if to say he hadn't a clue what everyone was talking about.

Little did Travis know that before the Screech Owls were back on a bus heading through the Fort Pitt Tunnel to the airport and home, he would dearly wish he did have a second head.

A spare head, sort of, that he could use to replace the one that no longer worked right.

2

"*Perfect!*" Sam and Sarah said simultaneously, their voices dripping with sarcasm.

"Whaddyamean by that?" a familiar voice squealed.

Travis turned around – not to identify the voice, which obviously belonged to Nish, but to see exactly *what* it was that Samantha Bennett and Sarah Cuthbertson were ridiculing. The Screech Owls were waiting to head out for their first practice, most of them sitting around the coffee shop in their hotel.

Travis first saw the two girls shaking their heads in disgust. Then he saw Nish.

Or, at least he presumed it was Nish. Whatever it was, it was wearing an ice-blue mask, which covered the eyes but couldn't disguise two puffy cheeks that were growing redder by the second.

Nish was not only wearing a mask, he had on this tight T-shirt, whitish blue, with a huge icicle forming the letter *I* splitting his chest in two.

"What could be better than a big *I* on you, Big Boy?" Sam shot.

The other Owls were giggling.

Nish looked about to burst. He tore his mask off and tossed it onto the nearest table, almost causing Fahd Noorizadeh's cherry Coke to tip into his lap. Fahd, who had never been known for his good hands in hockey, caught the drink just in time.

Nish's mouth moved as if it were trying to trap a bumblebee. "The *I*," he said, speaking very carefully and very loudly, "stands for ICEMAN! I am the new Iceman! And if you don't smarten up and shut up, I'll freeze you both solid!"

"Deal, Big Boy," laughed Sam, using an elastic to put her red hair into a ponytail. "We've been trying to freeze you out for years now."

The rest of the Owls roared. Nish slammed his thick fist down on the table – this time causing Fahd's cherry Coke to jump completely off the table and onto the floor. Nish grabbed his mask and stomped back toward the elevator.

"I'm going to get my equipment," he said in a defeated tone.

Sam took one last shot: "*Don't forget to thaw out your underwear, Mr. Iceman!*"

Travis hadn't seen this coming. Maybe Fahd might do it. Maybe Simon Milliken. But Wayne Nishikawa? *The Iceman?*

Though when he thought about it, there had been some signs. In the past few months, Nish had become obsessed with superheroes. He had all the X-Men videos, and had even taken up reading – mind you, comic books rather than real books, but reading all the same. This was a huge change for Nish, who had once told Travis that the only

possible use he could see for books was to use
them as goalposts while playing mini-stick hockey
in the basement.

Nish had convinced his poor suffering mother
to buy every superhero movie at Walmart and now
considered himself the world expert on Superman
and Batman and the Flash and Green Lantern and
Spider-Man and Wolverine and even Wonder
Woman. He knew about special powers, magic
rings, and bracelets. He knew all about the various
enemies – the Joker, Scorpion, Sabretooth. He
knew so much about the X-Men he could give
Data a run for his money. Larry Ulmar was called
Data by the Screech Owls because he seemed to
know everything about everything, so it was pretty
impressive to Travis that Nish could equal him.

Travis had never known his friend to show
such interest in new knowledge. It might be a little
weird, but at least Nish was finally learning something. His tiny little brain, it turned out, was actually capable of thinking about something other
than hockey and funny body sounds.

Travis had tried to figure it out. Nish still hadn't

made the *Guinness World Records* for any of his mad schemes, nor had he got himself displayed as a wax figure at Madame Tussauds. Maybe the superheroes were just another madcap plan to get him there.

Travis knew where the silly mask had come from. Mr. Dillinger had driven the team to the airport in his old bus, and on the way he had treated the Owls to one of his beloved Stupid Stops – this time at a huge variety store near the highway that sold everything, from fireworks to party hats, to the tourists heading north each summer to their cottages. Mr. D's rules were always the same: two dollars a player – once in a while as much as five dollars – and it had to be spent on something totally useless. That must have been where the shaving cream had come from that ended up on Travis's head. And the party section of the store was obviously where Nish had found that glittery blue and white "ice" mask.

At one point, Nish had even tried to explain his new obsession to Travis, with little result. "You see," Nish had said, "the thing is that most superheroes start out perfectly normal. Batman, for example – he's just a kid growing up who has a lot of money and a cave and decides he's going to live this secret life fighting crime. And Green Lantern, he was just this kid, Hal Jordan, who was given the magic ring and lantern by an alien he didn't know was an alien. And then you've got Bobby Drake. He's perfectly normal, too – fights with his family, has trouble at school – until one day he discovers by accident that he has this special power."

"What power?" Travis asked.

"He's out on his first date, and this bully dude tries to take his girlfriend away. So Bobby gets all angry. Now, you've got to understand that his anger is way different from Dr. Bruce Banner, another completely normal guy at the start, who gets angry and suddenly breaks out as the Incredible Hulk. Bobby has no idea what's going to happen. All he does is point at this bully dude to warn him and – poof! – the bully turns into a block of ice."

"He kills him?"

"Freezes him. Gets back his girl and moves on."

"What about the bully?"

"Who *cares* about the bully?"

"Well, you can't just walk around killing people you don't like. That's against the law."

Nish grinned from ear to ear, his face reddening. "I am the Iceman – I *am* the law!"

"You're nuts."

"If you believe in me, it will happen."

"I don't believe in you. You're talking nonsense."

"Say what you want," Nish said with supreme confidence. "*I am the Iceman, and I have superpowers!*"

"Okay," Travis said. "Show me."

"I can't," Nish said sheepishly. "I have to wait for them to show themselves to me. Once that happens, then I can show you."

Travis dropped it right there. It was too much. He was supposed to accept that Nish was a perfectly normal boy who was really a superhero-in-waiting, and that one day these magical powers would show up, and from then on he'd be a masked avenger whose mission was to save the world.

"I liked you better when you just wanted to moon everyone."

Nish grinned even wider. "Who says I have to give up one to do the other?"

"What do you mean?"

"The Iceman can still moon. *It's not like I'll freeze my butt off, is it?*"

3

Coach Muck Munro had called on an old friend from junior hockey who was now scouting for the Pittsburgh Penguins, and the friend had somehow arranged for the Owls to practice at the CONSOL Energy Center.

The Screech Owls were thrilled. This was "The rink that Sidney Crosby built" – a massive NHL rink high on the hill in the Uptown area of Pittsburgh, above the three rivers that from the air made the city look like a badly sliced pizza. When it opened, it was said to be the best hockey arena in the world. Had Mario Lemieux – number 66, "The Magnificent One" – not taken over owner-ship of the Penguins, and had the team not lucked into Sidney Crosby in the draft, there would have been no NHL team in the city. Now, however, thanks to Mario and Sidney and the star players who came along later, the team was considered a jewel in the NHL crown.

And what a jewel the arena was. Travis knew it was just a practice, but he treated it like Game 7 of the Stanley Cup final. He dressed in silence, put-ting on his pads in the right order, kissing his prac-tice jersey from the inside as he pulled it over his head, tapping his heart to feel the cloth of the cap-tain's *C* that he wore with such pride.

Mr. D had given his skates a fresh sharp, and Travis stepped carefully on the rubber mats as he made his way to the ice, walking as if he were about to break through the thin early-winter ice at his grand-parents' cottage. He didn't want to risk losing an edge.

Travis could hardly believe he was stepping out onto the same ice that Sidney Crosby had played on, the same ice that the great Mario Lemieux some-times skated on. He was first out. He cut around the first corner hard, his skates sizzling as he dug in. Then, to strengthen his ankles, he kept his legs together and "snaked" up the ice just by moving his feet in tandem with each other. He stepped out of his "snake" skate and looked back at the wavy paral-lel lines that his skates had left in the new ice. His mark would not last long – the other Owls were pouring out onto the ice with shouts of joy – but for a fleeting moment, Sidney Crosby's ice rink had only Travis Lindsay's mark on it. His *signature*.

Muck ran a smart practice. The Screech Owls did a few breakout drills, then some three-on-one rushes, then three-on-two. Some coaches ran rigid "systems" – you either took the puck up the ice exactly as instructed or you would be benched – but Muck said systems were for work, not play. He also said, "You invent this game every time you play it," which Travis took to mean that Muck wanted to see creativity. In Muck's book, the Owls should be ready to try whatever seemed possible, if they did so responsibly. So long as you stayed aware of what might happen if you lost the puck, you could pretty much attempt anything. No wonder the Owls loved playing for him.

As always at the end of practice, the Owls scrimmaged. In scrimmage, you could do anything you liked, and there was one play Travis had seen on the Internet that he wanted to try. A young Finnish player had gone behind the other team's net, used a scoop play with the blade of his stick to lift the puck up and hold it there, like a small circle of dough on the end of a paddle about to be put into the oven, and then turned the blade and hurled the puck backward into the net. The goal had counted, too – nothing illegal, just bizarre and crazy and . . . fun.

Muck had them playing four-on-four to create a little more open ice, meaning a little more time as well. Sarah, Travis, and Dmitri Yakushev had been working on a crisscross play in which Sarah, who had the puck at center, headed for Travis's left wing while Travis cut for center. But Sarah would simply leave the puck behind as she flew up the ice. With luck, it would fool the defense. They'd be trying to cut her off, only to realize, too late, that she no longer had the puck. Travis would go all the way over to Dmitri's wing, putting Travis on the off-wing, a left-hand shot on the right side, while Dmitri took over center. It gave Travis three options: he could pass all the way over to Sarah, he could try to use Dmitri for a tip, or he could shoot himself.

Sarah dropped the puck as planned, and Travis picked it up, faking a second drop pass to Dmitri as they cut across each other's paths. But Travis still had the puck and was coming down fast on Fahd, who was rapidly backpedaling, and on Nish, the other defenseman. Travis faked the shot and held, swooping around behind the net. He figured, "Why not?" and tried the scoop – and it worked! The puck was lying on his stick blade.

Travis looped hard around the net, neatly sidestepping Nish at the same time. He saw Jeremy Weathers move in goal to take away the shot from Dmitri, presuming Travis would try a back pass.

But Travis held the puck in the air, paused, then fired it back hard as if he were holding a lacrosse stick, not a hockey stick, and the puck flew into the side of the net just over Jeremy's shoulder.

"*No fair!*" Nish was screaming.

"*Illegal!*" shouted Fahd.

Travis and Sarah and Dmitri were all high-fiving and laughing as Jeremy dug the puck out of the back of his net. Nish, red-faced and glaring, was clearly upset at Travis's trick goal.

Muck came over, whistle dangling around his neck, his expression giving away nothing. It was impossible to tell if the coach was pleased or upset. Muck was always difficult to read.

"Just keep something like that to practice," he said to the three linemates. "We don't make a habit out of humiliating our opposition."

Message received and noted. Travis looked back at his coach and nodded.

And Muck winked.

He had enjoyed the little trick as much as anyone.

4

Muck's old hockey buddy had arranged a special rate for the Screech Owls, so for once they were put up in a hotel, three to a room, rather than being billeted out to families. Billeting had its good side – Travis had made several new friends that way – but being together was best. The Owls could eat together, hang out together, play together, and come and go from their games together.

The hotel was in Station Square, once the location of an old railroad station directly across the

Monongahela River from downtown Pittsburgh. Travis's room, which he shared with Nish and Fahd, looked out over the water and the riverboat casino, and if they cranked the window open, leaned out, and looked to their left, they could see old Fort Pitt where Pittsburgh's two rivers joined and, beyond that, the yellow bridges that took cars and pedestrians over to Three Rivers Stadium, where the Pirates played baseball in summer, and massive Heinz Field, the Steelers' football stadium, where the Peewee Winter Classic would be played.

Sarah, Sam, and Jenny Staples, the Owls' second goaltender, had a room on the other side, facing Mount Washington. It wasn't a true mountain, but it was still twice as steep as any hill around the Owls' hometown of Tamarack, which had its own tourist lookout called the Mountain.

Pittsburgh's Mount Washington had an interesting feature – a sort of elevator that rose on a steep track all the way up to the streets and restaurants on top of the high hill. Another one came down farther along Mount Washington just across from the sports fields. Travis had seen one before, called a funicular railway, which slowly moved up and down the cliffs of Quebec City while passengers looked out and felt their stomachs churn. In Pittsburgh, they were called Inclines, and the Owls could hardly wait to travel on them, whatever they were called.

Nish, as usual, wanted to be first into the room so he could stake out the best bed. Once the elevator stopped, he raced ahead down the hall of the recently refurbished hotel with his key card already out.

Travis and Fahd arrived at their hotel-room door to find their friend red-faced and gasping.

"I can't find where the key goes in!" Nish whined.

"Use your superpowers," Travis joked.

Nish sneered back at him, unimpressed.

"It's too dark," said Fahd. He brought out his cell phone and selected the light app to illuminate the door.

"There's no slot!" Nish said.

"We'll have to go back down," Travis said, trying to take a leadership role.

"What's up, boys?" a voice called from down the hall.

They turned to see a large woman by an open door with a bundle of sheets in her arms. Behind her was a cart she was loading with laundry.

"We can't get in!" Nish said as if the world were coming to an end here on the sixth floor of the Sheraton.

The woman laughed as she walked toward the three boys. She shook her head as if she'd seen this scene played out a dozen times.

"Watch," she said.

She pulled a key card from her belt, a retractable line stretching as she passed the key over the handle with a sweep.

The boys heard clicking and falling levers, then a quick buzz. The woman cranked the handle and the door opened like magic.

"Neat," said Travis.

"There's no slot," she said. "The door recognizes your card and opens automatically. Brand new, just last week."

"Open Sesame!" said Fahd, amazed.

"Wazzat mean?" asked a befuddled Nish.

"Ali Baba," Fahd explained, as if he couldn't believe Nish had never heard the expression.

"Who dat?"

"Ali Baba and the Forty Thieves," an exasperated Fahd continued. "That's how they opened the cave: *Open Sesame!*" He clapped his hands sharply to indicate it happened by magic.

"Ali Baba had magic powers?" Nish asked.

Fahd shook his head in disgust. "Obviously."

"Then the Iceman should know him . . ."

5

For the first match in the Peewee Winter Classic, the Screech Owls were scheduled to play a local team, the Pittsburgh River Rats, which meant there would be a good home crowd. Mr. D even said that the local television outlets would be there to interview players and shoot some of the action. The Owls were pumped.

They were to gather in the lobby. Nish – having claimed the best bed, having turned his mother's carefully packed suitcase upside down and dropped the contents all over the floor like a front-end loader dumping a load of dirt, having stunk out the bathroom and checked the window and the walkway below to see how it was set up for water bombs, having stashed his precious chocolate bar supply in a bottom drawer of the room's only dresser, having combed his hair four different ways in an attempt to look like Elvis Presley – was finally ready, and the three teammates made their way to the elevator and down to the lobby, where other Owls had already gathered.

"You are *not* going to believe this!" Sarah said when she saw Travis.

She seemed super excited. Her blue eyes were flashing. Travis raised his eyebrows and waited to be told the news.

"We think the Stanley Cup is here!" Sam practically shouted.

"What?" Travis said.

"*WHERE?*" Nish roared.

"Data says that's the guy who carries the cup," Dmitri said, pointing over toward the front desk, where there was a short lineup to register.

Travis thought he recognized one man waiting in line. He had seen him in commercials that had run all through the last Stanley Cup playoffs. Travis was almost certain he was the guy who put on white gloves and carried the trophy out onto the ice for the presentation. This was the Stanley Cup everyone recognized, but Travis, like the rest of the Owls, knew it wasn't the original – that historic trophy was on permanent display in the Hockey Hall of Fame. They knew this because they had been there when thieves tried to steal it. The Stanley Cup carried by the man in the white gloves was a replica, with silver rings added below it to hold the names of the players on the teams that won the championship. It was this Stanley Cup that the players hoisted when they won, and this Stanley Cup that the winning players and coaches were allowed to take to their home-towns for a single day during the summer. Travis had often seen photographs of those visits, and usually the guy standing in line at the hotel reception desk was there, too.

Travis saw Data wheeling in the Owls' direction. He was always amazed at how quickly Data could move his chair. There had been a time after the accident when Data had needed help getting anywhere in it, but no longer. Data was as mobile as anyone on the team and still very much a Screech Owl, even if he no longer played.

Data spun his chair to a sharp stop in front of Travis. He seemed very excited.

"I found it," Data said.

"Found what?" Travis asked.

"Come with me – but be quiet."

The small group of Owls, led by Data in his wheelchair, slipped quietly across the lobby to a luggage cart near the elevators. Across the top of the velvet-covered cart was a brass bar, and from the bar hung a plastic suit bag. Below it was a suitcase, and to one side was a large dark-blue box with silver handles, metal corners, and a heavy lock. Stamped on the box was "PROPERTY OF HOCKEY HALL OF FAME" complete with an address and telephone number.

Beside the luggage cart stood a bellhop.

Fahd couldn't resist. "Is that the Stanley Cup?" he asked the bellhop.

"No idea, young man," the bellhop said. "No idea at all."

The Owls turned their attention back to the front desk. The man they thought they recognized had his room key now and was walking toward the elevators. The bellhop was opening the elevator doors and pushing the cart in.

"Is that the cup?" Nish asked.

"What cup?" the man replied with a big smile.

"The Stanley Cup," Sam said in a voice that almost seemed slightly impatient.

"I don't know," said the man, still smiling. "What do you think?"

"We think it's the cup," said Travis.

"Ever seen it before?" the man said.

"We saw it when we went to the Hockey Hall of Fame," Sam said.

"I'm the guy who saved the original cup – the one they keep at the Hockey Hall of Fame," Nish shouted. "Wayne Nishikawa. N-I-S-H-I-K-A-W-A. I was in the papers!"

The man looked carefully at him, puzzled. "Then what's the big *I* for?" he asked, pointing at

Nish's superhero T-shirt. "*Wayne* doesn't begin with an *I* – nor does 'Nishikawa.' Is it the name of your team?"

"*I'm the Iceman!*" a red-faced Nish practically screamed.

"Our team is the Screech Owls," Travis told the man, who seemed oddly amused by Nish's ridiculous behavior.

"You must be in the Winter Classic, then," the man said as he stepped into the elevator behind the scowling bellhop.

"We are!" shouted Sam and Sarah together.

"Well, then," the man said. "Good luck."

"*Is that the Stanley Cup?*" Fahd shouted.

"Maybe," the man said with a wink. "Maybe it will show up at Heinz Field for the final. And just maybe the winners will have their pictures taken with it. But I'm not saying the Stanley Cup is or isn't in this box."

The Owls screamed in approval as the doors shut and the man, the bellhop, and the mysterious blue box were gone.

"Did we just learn that the winners are going

to get to raise the Stanley Cup?" Dmitri asked. "Just like in the NHL?"

"I believe so," said Sarah.

"*I saved the cup!*" Nish was shouting, his face about to burst with frustration.

No one paid him the slightest attention.

6

The Owls took the hotel shuttle across the closest yellow bridge, wound through downtown, and then took another bridge across to where the baseball park and the football stadium stood side by side at the large *Y* where the rivers met.

Muck had the shuttle driver stop in front of the baseball park and told the Owls to get out and gather on the sidewalk.

"We're a hockey team!" Nish protested. "Not a baseball team."

"Over this way," Muck said, ignoring the whining defenseman.

The coach led the way to a large bronze statue of a baseball player. It looked like he had just hit a home run, his left hand about to drop his bat to the ground, his legs already turned toward first base, his eyes watching an imaginary baseball sail through the sky toward the stands.

"This is Roberto Clemente," Muck said.

"Never heard of him," Nish muttered into his own shoulder. Muck still caught what he said.

"Well, you should," the coach said. "Fifteen times an all-star when he played for the Pirates. League MVP. MVP of the '71 World Series."

"Wow!" said Fahd.

"Impressive," added Data.

"But that's not why we're here," Muck continued. "MVPs in sport are a dime a dozen. It's MVPs in *life* that matter."

"Meaning . . . ?" Sarah asked.

"Roberto Clemente died trying to help people," Muck said. "He used his baseball fame and money to help his fellow Puerto Ricans, and

Latin Americans everywhere. He gave baseball equipment to kids too poor to buy gloves and bats and balls. He gave food to those who had none."

"How did he die?" Fahd asked.

"There was an earthquake in Nicaragua," Muck continued. "People were dying and desperately in need of help. Clemente chartered a plane and filled it with food and clothing, but it crashed into the sea right after takeoff. His body was never found. But his memory has never been forgotten, because he always put others ahead of himself. I want you to remember that. Now, back on the bus."

In stone silence, the Owls all walked back to the waiting vehicle. No one said a word. Nish, his face beet red and seemingly about to burst, was stopped from saying something stupid by a sharp jab in the gut from Sam's elbow.

As Travis took his seat for the remainder of the short ride to the frozen football stadium, he could not help but think of the man staring after the imaginary baseball. Roberto Clemente had every-thing anyone could ever dream of – fame, riches, the adoration of sports fans – and yet helping people he had never met from another country had been more important to him than all of that.

Travis vowed if he ever became a superstar in hockey – a Stanley Cup winner, a playoff MVP – he would never forget the lesson of Roberto Clemente.

Mr. D broke the silence as the shuttle came to a stop outside Heinz Field. "Let's go, Owls. We got us a game to win!"

7

"Sixty-five thousand and fifty," Data said, after Dmitri skated over and asked how many seats there were. "Six . . . five . . . zero . . . five . . . zero!"

Data sounded a little impatient, almost as if he couldn't believe Dmitri had forgotten. But Travis understood why Dmitri had asked: he hadn't forgotten at all, he just wanted to hear it out loud and let it sink in. *Sixty-five thousand and fifty . . .*

The Owls had played in front of big crowds before – at the Quebec International, at Nagano's

Big Hat arena, at the Olympic ice surface in Salt Lake City, at the world's biggest minor hockey tournament in Ottawa – but you could take all those impressive crowds together and sit them in Heinz Field and you would still have seats left over. Travis could not imagine so many people. He wondered how many would come to see the final. For the early rounds, the crowds would be small, and they'd seem even smaller in such a cavernous arena.

The Owls were already on the ice, Travis hurrying to pass Jeremy as soon as the little goaltender skated out ahead of him. Travis raced around, tapping the back of the net with his stick as he passed and digging in deep as he churned through the far corner. He could hear his skates roaring on the outdoor ice. He loved that sound. Different than indoors, always louder, almost as though the outdoor ice had a thin layer of brittle ice above an air pocket, where sound echoed as if in a tunnel. It was hard to describe. It was different, it was magnificent, it was magical.

Travis watched as the rest of his teammates spilled out of the doorway, each with his or her own special move as they hit the ice. Dmitri with his little stutter step; Sarah with her deep bow, touching one glove to the ice and then to her heart; Lars Johanssen looking up as if someone might be watching from the rafters, or in this case the clouds; and Nish doing his silly spinnerama on his second stride out, twirling around completely as if he were in a ballet instead of a game of hockey. Only this time there was something different about Nish. Something only his teammates knew. Beneath the red Screech Owls jersey, beneath the big *A* on his chest for Assistant Captain and the number 44 on his back with the name "NISHIKAWA," Nish was wearing his new superhero shirt.

The Iceman had come to play.

The Owls already had pucks in motion when the Pittsburgh River Rats took to the ice to the cheers and whistles of the crowd. The River Rats even had a high school marching band taking up three rows of seats behind their goal, and the band was louder than the fans.

Travis was ready. He clipped the crossbar on his very first shot in warm-up. Sarah was ready.

Travis had watched her, stick over her knees, bent over in the corner. He knew what she was doing: "envisioning" her first shift, imagining every single thing that would happen before it happened. Dmitri was ready. Travis slammed his stick down in salute as Dmitri went in, faked a shot, switched to his backhand, and roofed the puck over Jeremy's shoulder. Dmitri was always ready.

The referee blew his whistle for the starting lineups to come to center ice for the face-off. Travis felt a tingle go through his entire body as he took his position opposite the River Rats' big right-winger. The player was supposedly fast and tough, and Muck had said Travis would have to pay particular attention to him if the Owls were to keep him off the scoreboard. Travis liked an assignment like this just as much as scoring a goal or setting one up for Sarah or Dmitri.

Sarah looked at him, then at Dmitri, then back at Travis. He knew the signal. She would use a backhand swipe to try and send the puck ahead and to her left, onto Travis's wing. If he could beat the big winger, he'd have the puck heading into the River Rats' end.

The referee checked both goal lights. At each end of the temporary rink, the lights flashed back to show that the goal judge was in position and ready. The referee then slammed down the puck and jumped deftly back, turning on one skate as Sarah clipped the puck ahead on her backhand. The play had worked perfectly.

Travis was under the big winger's arm and away faster than the winger could turn.

He lost the puck temporarily but gathered it in his skates and kicked it ahead to his stick blade. The River Rats' right defenseman was trying to squeeze him off as he came across the blue line.

Travis and Sarah had a set play for this moment, too. As Travis bled the defender off toward the boards, he used his backhand to drive the puck into the boards just behind him. It made a different sound outside than if they had been playing indoors, more like a rifle shot than a muffled crack. The puck bounced off perfectly, and Sarah, coming up hard behind him, picked it off just as she crossed the line.

She had a clear channel to the net. She came down two-on-one with Dmitri and faked a saucer pass to her linemate, which caught the Rats' other defenseman off guard. He fell, thinking to block the quick pass, but Sarah kept on, and in an instant, there was no one but the goalie between her and the net. One quick fake to go to her backhand and she swept around the goalie and neatly slipped the puck into the net just under the falling goalie's right arm.

Screech Owls 1, River Rats 0.

"Nice drop," Sarah said, when the line returned to the Owls' bench.

"I thought you were going to pass to Dmitri," Travis said.

"So did I," Sarah smiled. "I meant to – so I had to score."

The two friends high-fived each other on the bench, Travis just catching Muck's disapproving eye as their gloves met. The Owls' coach didn't want to see any hotdogging, and certainly not from his captain.

Next shift, the face-off was in the Owls' end. Nish was on defense with Lars. Sarah got thrown out of the face-off circle for trying to swipe at the puck even before it dropped. Travis came in to take the draw. He won it cleanly back to Nish, who took the puck behind the Owls' net. Nish surveyed both sides, deciding on his best chance. For a flickering moment, Travis thought he could see Nish scanning the distant crowds in Heinz Field, as if imagining what he must look like as the center of attention, his favorite spot. But it was only for the slightest moment. Nish skated out the left side, looking for a play.

It was a perfect opportunity for the "crisscross" play Travis and Sarah had been working on in practice. It would also put Travis back on his wing and return Sarah to center. Travis knew Sarah would see him start it and follow suit. Just as he passed over the Owls' blue line, he cut hard in the opposite direction to the way everyone would be expecting him to go. He looked back, sure Nish would now try and hit him with the pass.

Travis felt an impact. Something hard against his back, punching against his helmet.

He saw the boards racing at him.

He could not turn, could not avoid what was coming, could not soften the blow.

He drove headfirst into the boards.
And then there was nothing but black.
Nothing.

8

They were trying to kill him.

They were using lights as weapons, stabbing him right through his eyeballs if he opened his eyelids so much as a crack. He wished they were sewn tight. He wished he could keep them still, but the sheer effort of clamping his eyelids shut caused them to shake and flutter and pop open – no matter how hard he fought to prevent it.

The light sent pain shooting through his skull. It was as if tiny hand grenades were going off inside his brain, his skull bouncing the shock waves around in his head like the walls of a pinball machine.

He tried to sit up. He felt the room spinning. He felt sick – *seasick* sick, just like that time his Uncle Simon took the family sailing on the Great Lakes and they hit heavy swells an hour away from shore. It had been the worst feeling Travis had ever known: a gut-wrenching, disoriented feeling that, his uncle joked, was "a thousand times worse than death."

He lay back and the nausea passed. He kept his eyelids shut as tight as the lids on the jars of strawberry jam his grandmother put up each summer, and the pain in his head slowly went away.

What is wrong with me? Travis asked himself. *What happened?*

"You have suffered a concussion."

The room was still dark, but not entirely dark. Travis half-opened his eyes. A man he did not know was sitting on the bed. He had a stethoscope hanging over his left shoulder. Travis presumed he was a doctor. Standing behind him was Mr. D, and behind Mr. D was Muck.

"The good news is you have no other damage," the doctor continued. "But no more hockey for you for a while, young man. Mr. Dillinger will make sure that you're a hundred percent recovered before you return to play. You'll have to be cleared by your doctor back home before you get back on skates."

Travis tried to speak but could not. He cleared his throat and tried again. "W-w-what happened?"

The doctor was already packing up his stuff. Mr. D came and sat in the spot where the doctor had been. He moved so carefully he settled on the bed as softly as a butterfly on a flower.

"You got coldcocked, Trav," Mr. D began. "Actually, both of you did, but the big winger on the River Rats didn't hit the boards like you did. But he still went down hard, I can tell you that." Mr. D suppressed a small chuckle, almost as though he was proud of Travis for holding his own in the on-ice collision.

Muck jumped in, speaking very quietly, as if he knew loud noise could be as painful to Travis as sharp light. "You cut across to get back on your wing just as he was cutting left to try and catch Sarah. You turned as you neared the boards in case Nish was looking to pass to you. Both of you had blind spots. He wasn't trying to hit you or anything – it just happened."

"They took you off on a stretcher," Mr. D added. "So you can thank your lucky stars there were top-notch medical people there."

"I don't remember anything."

Mr. D seemed surprised. "You were alert when they put you in the ambulance. They took you to the hospital for X-rays and kept you over-night for observation. Standard procedure. You don't remember?"

The doctor paused, putting away his stetho-scope. "Short-term memory loss," he said, more to Muck and Mr. D than to Travis. "It's not at all uncommon. Has your team done baseline testing?"

"Yes," Mr. D said. "We do it each year at the first practice."

"Good, then your doctors back home will have something to measure his recovery by. He should be fine. Just keep him quiet and comfortable until you're heading home. Have someone check on him every hour or so. He'll just want to rest and sleep. No TV, no reading, no loud noises."

"That eliminates Nish," Mr. D chuckled. "We've moved your roommates out, Trav, so you'll have this place all to yourself. Muck and I have keys, so we'll be able to check on you without disturbing you."

Travis was wondering how much of his memory had gone when, suddenly, part of it jumped back. The Owls had been up 1–0 when he went down.

"Who won?" he asked.

"You guys did," Muck answered. "Some goofball defenseman who wants me to call him the Iceman put it away in overtime: 5–4 for the Owls."

"Your clothes are in the dresser there, Trav," said Mr. D. "But one of the drawers is full of candy bars. They yours, too?"

Nish's stash. The Iceman's power bars. A chance to get back at Nish.

"Yeah," Travis fibbed. "Leave 'em, please."

"Okay."

Travis started to giggle at his little trick while Muck and Mr. D followed the doctor out into the hall. As the three men talked quietly outside, sharp light poured in through the open door and directly into Travis's eyes.

The pain was excruciating. He felt tears flood his eyes.

Then the door closed and all was dark again.

9

Travis would enjoy this, Sarah thought, as the yellow school bus carrying the Screech Owls joined the convoy of yellow school buses heading south of Pittsburgh toward a small town called Shanksville.

She was sitting with Sam, and while Sam dozed off in the heat of the bus, Sarah stared out at the bare trees with their light covering of snow.

She had much to think about. She was worried about Travis, now into his second day of almost total isolation in his hotel room. She knew from reports from Mr. Dillinger that Travis was eating fine and resting well, that the doctor had been back to see him and was satisfied with his progress, that Travis was able to tolerate some light in the room and had even tried a half hour of television. He had wanted to watch a hockey game – the Penguins against the Washington Capitals – but the speed of the game and the quick cuts from camera to camera brought back the seasick feeling and he'd had to turn it off.

How awful, she thought. Unable to watch television. Unable to read. Unable to walk around outside. Just hours and hours of lying in a dark room waiting for your brain to get better.

But what could anyone have done to prevent it? Sarah knew about concussions in hockey. Every player did. Sidney Crosby's concussion, which had kept him from playing for most of a year, had made everyone see the dangers of head shots. For the most part – with tougher rules, more education – they were gone from minor hockey, but accidents could never be eliminated. Hockey was a fast game played on hard surfaces. Travis was lucky he hadn't been hurt far worse. It could have been a broken neck, and still it would have been an accident – no one's fault.

The Owls had continued in the tournament, winning a close game against a team from Philadelphia and then coasting to victory over the Little Devils, a peewee team from New Jersey that modeled their team colors and crest on the NHL's Devils. The Little Devils weren't nearly the match Philadelphia's Peewee Phantoms had been. In fact, if it hadn't been for one lucky bounce, the Phantoms might have beaten the Owls.

After the win over the Little Devils, Sarah and Sam had come out of the Owls' dressing room to find the River Rats player who had hit Travis waiting outside with his coach. The coach give the big kid a nudge on the back, sending him toward the girls.

The player looked like he was about to cry. He was twisting his hands together as if washing them. He seemed unable to look them in the eye. He stopped, fumbling for words.

"You're his center, right?" the big kid said to Sarah.

"Travis's? Yeah."

"How is he?"

"He'll be okay. He's just not allowed to play for a while."

"Can you give him this for me, please?" the kid asked, nervously handing over a folded note.

Sarah took it. She smiled at the big, fumbling kid. "Sure. Be glad to."

She knew she shouldn't have, but later, when she found herself alone in the lobby of their hotel, she couldn't resist taking the note from her pocket and reading it quickly.

Dear Travis,

I am very, very sorry for what happened to you. I am the kid who hit you into the boards. I didn't mean for it to happen and I feel terrible about it. If it means anything to you, I was almost knocked out myself – you are not only a very good player but a solid one as well. I hope you can forgive me.

Your friend,
Billy Chester

Almost in tears, Sarah tucked the note back into her pocket. When she saw Mr. Dillinger, she handed it over and asked him to give it to Travis when he next checked on the injured player. She hoped Travis was able to read. She knew he'd like hearing that he was not only a good player but a tough one.

There was light snow on the roads as the buses wound their way through the hilly countryside near Shanksville. The players were being brought to a field in what seemed like the middle of nowhere.

But it was definitely not nowhere. It was where United Airlines Flight 93 had crashed on September 11, 2001.

10

If Sarah hadn't known better, she'd have thought Muck had set this up. The Screech Owls' coach was always going on about history and the importance of remembering.

But this had nothing to do with Muck. The organizers of the Peewee Winter Classic had come up with this one all on their own. There were plenty of things to see in Pittsburgh – the children's museum, the science center, the Andy Warhol Museum – but they chose the field near

Shanksville where Flight 93 had crashed on 9/11.

The buses pulled into a freshly plowed parking lot, and slowly and quietly the various teams climbed down from their rides and gathered in small groups along the side. Sarah saw that the Pittsburgh River Rats had been on the bus directly behind theirs, and she made sure to catch Billy Chester's eye and give him a smile and a thumbs-up. He seemed relieved and smiled shyly back and waved.

A cold wind was blowing across the field. It picked up tiny wisps of snow like ghostly lassos and sent them whirling. But no one felt cold. And if they shivered, it wasn't because of the wind.

Sarah thought she was going to lose her breath as she walked along the memorial wall, a long line of ghostly white marble slabs with nothing on them but name after name after name. It had nothing to do with exertion; it was seeing all the names of those who had died and realizing they were real people who could never have imagined the horror awaiting them when their early morning flight took off from Newark, New Jersey.

A guide gave them a short talk on what had happened. Shortly after takeoff on a flight to San Francisco, the plane had been hijacked by four al-Qaeda terrorists using razor-sharp box cutters as weapons. Some of the passengers had cell phones and were using them to call home. That's how they learned they were not alone in whatever was happening. Two other hijacked planes had already slammed into the World Trade Center in New York City. A third plane hit the Pentagon in Washington, D.C. From the route taken by the hijackers of Flight 93, the authorities could tell that this plane was targeting either the White House or the United States Capitol.

The terrorists' plan was astonishing, both in its simplicity and in its intended goal. Using simple weapons, the men had easily taken over four regular flights. Each group of terrorists had one or two trained pilots among them who would take over the controls. Two planes would destroy the twin towers of the World Trade Center, symbol of the financial power of the United States of America. One plane would hit the military center of America, the Pentagon. And the fourth plane, Flight 93, was to strike at the very heart of the American political system and might have killed the president of the United States.

There were forty passengers and crew on Flight 93. When they realized what was happening in New York City and Washington, they knew that the hijackers were on a suicide mission and vowed that their plane would not be used the same way. They voted among themselves and decided to rush the cockpit, regardless of the consequences. They would bring the plane down themselves if need be.

This moment, the guide said, marked a turning point in the war against terrorism. It was the moment when ordinary people – people who could be your own neighbors, or your teachers, or your relatives – decided to fight back.

Todd Beamer, one of the passengers who decided to storm the cockpit, had been on the phone to a dispatcher on the ground. The last thing the dispatcher heard him say was addressed to the others around him: "Are you guys ready? Okay, let's roll."

"*Let's roll*," the guide repeated, pausing.

He did not repeat it again. He did not need to.

Sarah felt Sam's hand groping for hers. She took Sam's hand and held it tight, but no matter how hard she tried to stop it from happening, tears squeezed through her eyelids.

11

Travis thought he was losing his memory. Or perhaps he just had nothing to remember. It was starting to confuse him, scare him.

How many days had he been lying here? How many meals had he eaten? What had he eaten last? Was it lunch next? Or dinner?

He had tried watching television and could get through an hour or so before the pain started up again. He had brought one of the Harry Potter books with him and was able to read nearly a chapter before the headaches made him want to shut his eyes and lie in the dark. He'd got up several times and was now able to move about the room and washroom, slowly, without feeling nauseous. He was getting better – but was it ever going slow.

Was it afternoon? Or night? He couldn't tell with the heavy curtains drawn. And he didn't want to chance looking out and discover it was midday, with the sun at its brightest. He knew only too well how painful that could be. He'd already tried it a couple of times and quickly whisked the curtains back so they darkened the room once more.

Mainly, he lay in bed, eyes closed, mind wandering. He wondered how the tournament was going for the Owls. He wondered how little Simon Milliken was doing playing in his spot. He wanted Simon to play well, for the team's sake, for the sake of Sarah and Dmitri, his linemates, and also for Simon's sake, as he liked the guy a lot. But if he was being totally honest with himself, he sort of wanted the line to be struggling. He wanted the Owls to miss him as much as he missed them. He was, after all, their captain.

Where had they gone? he wondered. Mr. D had called in earlier and said something about a team outing somewhere. He couldn't remember where.

He felt himself drifting off. He had crazy thoughts, or were they dreams? He was failing at school and couldn't do a test; he was trying to skate but had no skates on, and no one else could see he was struggling in his boots, unable to keep up with the others; he was Spider-Man, and Nish really was the Iceman, and they were rounding up bad guys to turn them over to the police to be put in jail.

He heard voices. Voices inside his head? From somewhere else? Men talking. Men arguing. Getting louder and louder and louder, until Travis thought his head was going to split.

He needed a drink of water. He was getting delirious. He was maybe going to be sick again.

Travis struggled out of bed and eased himself to his feet. He began moving very slowly toward the bathroom.

There were the voices again. Louder now.

"*Sunday morning!*" one yelled.

"*I say tonight!*" another shouted back.

"It's all set up for Sunday morning!"

Travis stopped, listening. These weren't voices in his head. They were real. Real voices coming from the room next door.

There was a doorway between Travis's room and the next one. It was a double door, locked on both sides. Travis knew this because, of course, it was one of the first things Nish had checked when they arrived. Nish was convinced that if he could slip into another room, he might be able to look at an adult movie and have the charge go to someone else's bill.

The voices dropped, becoming more of a murmur, but every so often a word or two came through the closed door.

"No!"

"We do as Bert says!"

"This is a joke!"

Travis remembered – yes, *remembered*, it made him smile with relief – a trick Data had taught them when the Owls were convinced a girls' ringette team had taken over the suite beside them in a motel.

The boys had heard giggling and were trying to listen through the wall to whatever it was the girls were saying. They hadn't had much luck until Data went into the washroom and returned with a drinking glass. He moved his wheelchair up tight to the wall, placed the bottom of the glass against his ear, and pressed the other end hard against the wall.

Data told them every word the girls were saying. They were talking about boys, he said. But none of them was called Travis or Lars or Nish or Jesse Highboy or Derek Dillinger or any other name belonging to a Screech Owl.

Travis made his way to the washroom and found a glass neatly wrapped in paper. He undid the paper and returned to the door with the glass, placing it against his ear and then pressing tight enough to the door that the glass was snug against the wood.

The voices were clearer now.

"It's the key, dammit," one of the men was saying. "We won't be able to get it until Sunday morning, and then we'll only have an hour or so to pull it off."

Pull what off? Travis wondered.

The other voice was angry. "This is *not* something you want to do in broad daylight," he said. "We'll be seen."

"Can't," the first man said. "And we can't do it the night before, or tonight, because we don't have access to the key."

"How do you know we will Sunday morning?"

"Weekend shift for the staff. Our man will be in early and will make it so the key doesn't work. When the guy comes down to get his key re-coded, our man will be the one doing it, and he'll make a copy for us."

"Can we trust this person?"

"He's being well paid."

"Then what? How do we get it out of here without being seen? You've seen the parking area. There's no place you can conceal something like that."

"We won't be using the parking lot."

"How, then?"

"We go down the fire exit, then around the corner of the building. It'll be in a duffel bag and our man will be carrying a hockey stick – people will think he's heading off to play somewhere. He'll take the Incline up Mount Washington, and you'll be up there waiting with the car. It's simple."

"Sounds dangerous."

"You got a better idea?"

"I guess not."

Travis let the glass slip and it crashed on the edge of the dresser, shattering loudly. Immediately the voices stopped. He could hear the door to the room opening, then banging closed, as if someone was going out for a while.

Careful not to cut himself, he picked up the pieces of glass as best he could, wrapped them in the paper the glass had come in, and dumped them into the garbage in the bathroom.

What had he heard? What had all that been about? What were they doing with someone else's key? What did the man mean when he said they'd have "it" in a duffel bag and some guy would be pretending to be a hockey player?

And what was that about the Incline and the car up top? There was no rink up there, was there? He wouldn't really be going to play hockey, would he?

Travis's stomach growled. He was getting hungry. He craved a snack of some sort, only there was nothing in the room.

But wait a minute. *Nish's chocolate stash!* Travis went back to the dresser and yanked open the lowest drawer. They were still here. He grabbed a Mars bar and went back to sit on the bed, slowly unwrapping the bar and even more slowly chewing the rich, thick chocolate candy.

He had *remembered* something. Nish's stash. That was a good sign.

But what had just happened here? Had he really overheard some conversation about plans to steal something from the hotel?

Maybe it had all been a dream. He'd been having crazy dreams ever since the concussion.

It must have been a dream.

12

"You're *not* going to believe this!"

Sam's face was nearly the color of her carrot hair. She seemed shocked and delighted at the same time – her expressive face twisting between amusement and alarm as she raised a hand to indicate Sarah should follow her.

The Screech Owls were having a light practice skate. Muck wanted to make sure they kept sharp as they waited to find out which team they would meet in the semifinals. So far, the tournament had

gone well for them: two wins following the overtime victory against the River Rats.

Sam was leading the way, twisting through an
equipment room toward the ice surface. Sarah could
"feel" the ice in the air, the cold coming in through the
door Sam had opened. The colder the air, the better
the ice – and Sarah liked the coldness of this rink.

"Look at that!" Sam said, pointing.

Sarah heard it before she saw it: the sweet sound
of a good skater – like the sizzle of a frying pan –
cutting through a corner on fresh-flooded ice.

She moved quickly to the boards behind the
players' bench and stopped fast. *She couldn't possi-
bly be seeing what she was seeing.*

It was Nish. At least, she presumed it was Nish.

It was certainly Nish's body: there was no mis-
taking that chubby thing rounding the corner. He
was wearing Jeremy's new goalie mask with the
Screech Owls crest painted over it.

And the mask was pretty much *all* he was
wearing. He had tied a sheet around his neck, and
it flowed back like a great cape, a flag flapping in
the wind he was making.

He had on his skates . . . and his disgusting, frayed old gauchies. Skates, mask, underwear, cape – and not a single thing else.

"*Hey! Fat boy!*" Sam yelled. She called him over with a gesture that looked like she was splashing water in her face. Almost as if she were trying to wake herself from a bad dream.

Nish skated over, stopping hard in a shower of snow, some of which cleared the boards and landed on the two laughing girls.

"*What makes you think it is me?*" Nish asked in a fake voice from behind Jeremy's mask.

"Who else would be so stupid?" Sam shot back.

"What are you *doing*?" Sarah asked.

"Practicing," Nish said, using his normal voice. "Muck called a practice, so I'm practicing."

"Practicing for *what*?" Sam demanded.

"I'm going to streak the final," Nish said, matter-of-factly. "If there's fifty thousand people in the stands, I'll make the *Guinness World Records*."

"As what?" Sam sneered. "The world's stupidest kid?"

"Laugh if you like," Nish said. "I'll streak and I'll moon them – and no one will ever know it was me."

"Then how will you get in the *Guinness* book?" Sarah asked.

Nish pushed back Jeremy's mask and winced, his red face steaming like a cooked lobster.

"My cape," he said, smiling smugly. He reached back and pulled the sheet up. "This will have a huge *I* on it, for 'Iceman.'"

"And people will know that?" Sarah asked. "You honestly think that people in the stands will know you're supposed to be the Iceman?"

"Not *supposed to be.* I *am* the Iceman!"

"They still won't know who you are. All they'll see is some sick kid in a goalie mask and an old sheet."

"Then I won't have a mask," Nish argued. "I don't have to wear it. You watch! I'll do it Sunday in the final."

"Thanks all the same," Sarah said, turning to go. "But we'd rather not watch."

Nish snapped the goalie mask back down in place and took off, his sheet snapping behind him in the quick wind, then dropping down and entangling in his skate.

He went down with a thud, spinning on his stomach toward the far net.

The girls were in pain they were laughing so hard. Sarah could barely speak.

"Good thing the Iceman is wearing those gauchies!"

13

Travis woke with a start.

Where was he? Oh yeah, Pittsburgh. What time was it? Heck, what *day* was it?

He lay with his head cradled deep in a pillow, not moving. Every time he opened his eyes in the semidarkness, it was as if new information flowed into his brain. It slowly came back. The injury. The doctors. The quiet room. The closed curtains. The slow but sure recovery. It no longer made him dizzy to sit up. He no longer felt ill walking to the washroom. He was eating well and hungry again. *Breakfast? Lunch? Dinner?* He wasn't certain which one was next.

He felt a lot better, but it seemed he'd been dreaming far more than he'd been awake the past few days. Some of the dreams had been silly – a dog that could talk, jet-propelled hockey skates, a permanent, year-round rink in his backyard – and some had been frightening – his head splitting open from pain, his family lost, him never playing hockey again.

The sound of a door slamming in the hall reminded him of another door being banged, and then another dream he'd had came flooding back. The argument about what day to do something. The talk about the key that would be copied. The plan to use the Incline up Mount Washington so as not to be noticed. The guy faking he was just a hockey player carrying his stick and equipment bag off to practice or a game.

It made no sense. It had to be another of those silly dreams.

Travis got up and went to the window to pull back the curtains. He winced when the sharp sunlight poured in, but there was no pain. There was no pain, no nausea, no sense that he needed to lie back down right away in the dark.

His eyes slowly adjusted and he looked out. He could see down toward the river and across to the city of Pittsburgh. He felt truly good for the first time since he had been knocked cold. He wanted to go out. It was the first time he had felt this, and it made him smile.

He was getting better. And getting better fast. Maybe, he thought, he could even play if the Screech Owls were still alive in the tournament. But then he remembered what the doctor had said, how he needed to be cleared by his own doctor back in Tamarack. He knew Muck and Mr. D would never do something so foolish as to put an injured player back in the lineup.

He turned to go to the washroom and jumped back. A pain like fire shot through his foot.

He sat on the edge of the bed and looked down. In the light streaming in through the window, something sparkled on the bottom of his foot. Travis brushed lightly at his naked heel and the pain shot through his foot again. He could see something sticking into his heel.

A shard of glass.

Ever so carefully, Travis pinched the sliver of glass between his thumb and forefinger and pulled it free. It slipped out easily, and a small drop of blood beaded on his heel. He reached for a tissue and dabbed it. There was no more blood. He put his foot down on the floor and stood again. There was no more pain. He had got all the glass out.

Where had it come from? And then he remembered.

He went into the washroom and checked the garbage can. In the bottom was a little paper parcel, and wrapped inside the paper were the jagged pieces of a broken water glass.

Another memory exploded in his brain. He got up and almost ran to the dresser to pull out the lowest drawer.

It was filled with chocolate bars. Nish's stash. But one had been eaten: a Mars bar wrapper was off to the side. Travis knew he'd eaten that bar, and he knew when.

The chocolate bar, the glass he had used to listen in on the strange conversation in the next room. It hadn't been a dream. He really had heard it. The men really had been planning something.

But what?

14

It was Saturday, the second-last day of the Peewee Winter Classic, and the Screech Owls were one game away from the final. They had played exceptionally well, even without Travis Lindsay in the lineup, but now they were about to meet the Portland Panthers to decide who got to play for the Winter Classic championship.

The Owls knew the Panthers well. They had beaten them and been beaten by them in past tournaments. They had even got to know some of the players – Jeremy Billings, the slick little defense-man, and Stu Yantha, the tall and powerful center – and had come to like and respect them.

Sarah was wearing the *C*. She had worn it before, so this was nothing new. She'd been the Owls' first captain, but the *C* had gone to Travis when she went to play for an all-girls team, and it had stayed with Travis after she returned. They were *both* team leaders, and if there could have been two *C*'s, Sarah and Travis would have been the two Owls wearing them.

She was beside Sam, the two of them dressing quietly in the huge football-team dressing room at Heinz Field. The other Screech Owls were scattered about, none of them – not even Nish – talking while they readied themselves for what they knew was going to be a very tough, hard-fought game.

Most were fully dressed and finishing up tightening their skates when Muck came in and stood at the center of the room. It seemed he was about to make one of his special "speeches" – always using as few words as possible, always seeming slightly taken aback that he had to say anything at all. Muck wasn't one for inspirational speeches. He also believed that players decided games, not coaches. He was unusual in that way, and the Owls loved him for it.

Muck cleared his throat.

"It's a big game, kids. You know that. You don't need to be told what to do or what to think. You know what to do, and if you haven't already been thinking about this all day, you're not hockey players. You don't need any more coaches than you already have – but this game we're going to add one, if you don't mind."

"Who?" Fahd cried out.

Muck gave him a withering look. He then turned to the door, where Mr. Dillinger was standing with a grip on the handle.

Mr. D opened the door and in walked Travis. He was wearing his Screech Owls tracksuit and he was smiling through a deep blush.

The Owls' dressing room burst into cheers and screams of "*Travis!*" They rushed their red-faced little captain, high-fiving and fist-rapping with him, all of them so excited to see him back he couldn't get a word in himself.

Mr. Dillinger put his fingers in his mouth and blew his trademark shrill whistle.

"Listen up, now!" he shouted. "Travis will be on the bench this game, but he won't be able to play until we get back home and he gets cleared. But he's feeling good enough to be out, and the doctor here checked him over and says he's doing just fine. So, let's get out there and get into the big game, okay? That's what we came here for!"

"For Travis!" Sam shouted.

"*Travis!*" the other Owls screamed.

Travis made his way to the visitors' bench and sat in his usual place. He stuffed his hands in his tracksuit pockets and took in the sights. There were thousands in the stands, but they still looked empty. The rink in front of him looked tiny, shrunken, out of all proportion to the football stadium surroundings, but he knew it was just an optical illusion. The rink was regulation size. It was the stands that were Olympian.

The Owls were flying about the ice in a quick warm-up. Travis wished he could be out there with them. He watched Sarah take the far corner so fast her jersey snapped like a flag in the wind. He watched Nish dancing forward, backward, forward, backward in quick succession – the Iceman making sure his pivot was good and the edges of his skate blades right. Mr. Dillinger had done his usual perfect job of sharpening.

"Hey, Travis!" someone called. Travis looked toward the home bench and saw little Billings making his way along the boards.

Billings stopped in front of the Owls' bench. "I heard you got hurt," he said. "Okay now?"

Travis nodded. "I'm good."

"Good man," Billings said, reaching his stick out to tap Travis lightly. "See you back on the ice soon."

Travis just nodded. He was so struck by Billings's little gesture with the stick that he could hardly swallow, let alone speak.

The officials called for the game to start. Sarah came in opposite big Yantha at the face-off, and

Yantha, just as Billings had done, reached over and gently tapped Sarah's pads.

"Good game," he said.

"You, too," said Sarah.

And it was a fabulous game, the puck moving fast all over the ice, the crowd much louder than Travis had expected, given the size of the stadium and the distance they were away from the action.

Billings and Yantha combined on the first goal when Billings joined the rush, and Yantha simply dropped the puck in the slot and used his size to plow through Fahd and Lars on defense. Billings's quick, accurate shot beat Jenny five-hole. She got up fast and swung her stick hard against the far post. But it hadn't been her fault. No one could have stopped such a quick, hard shot.

With the Panthers up 3–2 heading into the final period, Dmitri knocked down a pass from the Portland defense and broke in alone, his familiar forehand-backhand move twisting the Panthers goaltender out of the crease, and his backhand sending the water bottle flying.

With five minutes left on the clock, Derek Dillinger and Andy Higgins broke away on a two-on-one, Billings the only Panther back. Derek had the puck and went to pass to Andy, waiting to one-time his shot, when Billings made a brilliant play by suddenly lunging forward between the two Owls and blocking the pass.

Unfortunately for Billings, the pass hit his shin pads and bounced right back to Derek. Because the Panthers' goaltender had also played the pass, anticipating a shot from Andy, Derek was left with a virtually empty net, and he easily fired in the goal that put the Owls up 4–3.

Travis felt sorry for Billings. It had been a brilliant defensive play, but as so often happened in hockey, the bounce went one way rather than the other. "Puck luck," Muck liked to call it. There were some things in hockey that no amount of skill could make happen and no amount of coaching could prevent. Puck luck.

The next five minutes Travis found harder than if he'd been playing. He tried to be useful by opening and closing the gate for the forwards, but most of the Owls were so pumped up they leaped the boards to get on and leaped them again to come off. He felt useless. But he was sweating harder than if he'd been playing. The tension was huge.

The Owls had only to hang on and they'd have their trip to the championship game. Though Muck had said in his speech that there wasn't much coaching he could do in a game like this, Travis thought that Muck was the key.

Muck kept sending out Nish with Lars, using his top defenders to keep the Panthers at bay. And he had Sarah staying back on her own side of center, always ready to back-check if necessary.

When those three tired to the point where none of them could go on, Muck called his time out. Though Muck had called it, however, he never said a word to his players. No lecture. No chalkboard to design a play. Nothing. Over at the Panthers' bench, their coach was taking the opportunity to do all of these things, rapidly drawing up plays and wiping the board clean and then trying another plan.

Travis laughed to himself. You would never have known it was Muck who called the time out.

He looked at Nish, bent almost double on the ice, gasping for breath. His tomato face looked about to explode. How could Nish be the most thoughtless, ridiculous person on earth, Travis wondered, and also be the most dependable, most determined defenseman on the team? It was as if he were two different people. And today, in fact he was: "Nishikawa" might have been the name on his jersey, but underneath was the Iceman T-shirt.

The time out over, the referee blew his whistle and called the teams back to the face-off circle. It would be Sarah against Yantha. She looked up, waiting for the linesman to drop the puck.

Yantha winked.

They both knew this was a great game. They both knew that one team would go on and the other would go home. But there was no dislike, only admiration. If the Panthers won, Sarah would cheer for them; if the Owls won, Yantha had just told her without saying a word, the Panthers would do the same.

Yantha won the face-off and got away a quick shot that rang off the crossbar behind Jenny and into the glass and out of play.

They faced off again, and this time Sarah won, sliding the puck back to Nish, who calmly took it behind his own net.

He was killing time, staring up at the clock, which seemed, to Travis, to be moving slower than a snail. *Hurry up!* he said to himself. *Hurry up!*

Nish worked his way out of his own end, carefully protecting the puck. He dumped it in, and the Owls waited at center for the attack, led by little Billings.

The Panthers came on strong. Billings had a good shot from the point and Yantha a second chance on the rebound, but Jenny was acrobatic in the Owls' net and kept both shots out.

With a minute and a half to go, the Panthers pulled their goalie. He raced off as another Panther rolled over the boards.

With a player advantage, the Panthers pressed

even harder, but a combination of Nish blocking shots and Jenny stopping them meant they couldn't score.

Finally, Billings drove a hard shot that a falling Nish took off his shin pads.

Even falling, Nish was able to sweep the puck out over the blue line, where Dmitri, with his blazing speed, was able to gobble it up. He got it across to little Simon Milliken, who skated in all alone and dropped the puck into the Panthers' net.

A 5–3 victory for the Screech Owls.

The Owls mobbed Simon, and when Simon came to the bench, Travis thought the little guy was almost in tears. Tears of joy.

It crossed Travis's mind that it would have been him out there, not Simon, if he hadn't been hurt – that he would be the hero being mobbed. But he shook off the thought. He was glad for Simon.

The clock ran down quickly after the final face-off. When the buzzer sounded, Travis watched as Yantha went over and tapped Sarah's shin pads and she tapped his back.

They lined up to shake hands, and when the handshakes were done, Billings led the Panthers over to the Owls' bench, where each of them in turn leaned over the boards to shake Travis's hand.

"Next time," Billings said with a smile.

"Next time," Travis smiled back.

15

"**I** need to talk to you."

Travis had taken Sarah aside as soon as the victorious Owls had returned to Station Square. They had been singing and laughing on the bus, but Sarah had noticed that Travis sat quietly on his own, staring out at the river as the shuttle carrying the team crossed the bridges and twisted through the streets. She figured it was for good reason – he was better, but not completely recovered from the concussion. Besides, Travis was naturally quiet. As her father often said of those who spoke little, "Still waters run deep." And that pretty much summed up Travis Lindsay in her mind.

But now he wanted to talk.

"Shoot," she told him, but he shook his head.

"Not here."

"We can walk down along the river," Sarah suggested. "I'll get my coat and meet you in the lobby."

"Bring Sam," he said.

Sarah nodded and headed for the elevator. What could all this be about? she wondered as the elevator doors closed.

Travis went up to his room for his own coat. He pulled his bulky team jacket over his tracksuit and was just leaving again when Nish – the Iceman – came running along the hallway so as to make the sheet with the big *I* on it fly out behind him like a real cape. The sheet was frayed. Nish had clearly been working at it with scissors, trying to get it to a size where it wouldn't trip him up on his skates.

Nish stopped, and the cape fell around his shoulders and dangled as far as his knees. He was puffing.

"Wazzup?" he asked.

"I'm just going down to meet Sarah. We're going for a walk."

"Can I come?"

Travis swallowed. He had originally thought to tell only Sarah. He imagined that the two of them, as captain and assistant, might go to Mr. Dillinger for advice on what to do. But he'd already told Sarah to bring Sam along.

"I guess," Travis said.

He knew if he said no, there would be no end to the teasing from his big-mouth friend. Nish would carry on as if Travis and Sarah were going off for some romantic stroll in the moonlight, which wasn't the case at all. It wouldn't stop Nish from teasing, though.

There was a sharp wind coming in off the river. The Owls all had their jackets zipped tight to the throat and hats pulled down over their ears. Nish, with no gloves, had his hands stuffed deep into his jacket pockets.

A light snow swirled across the water. The river looked cold and gray. Much better, Travis thought, for lakes and rivers to freeze hard, as they had back home. He didn't like this damp cold and half wished they'd just met to talk in one of the fast-food outlets in the square.

But he didn't want anyone else to hear. Not yet, anyway. Not until he knew what he had. Or could accept that in reality he had nothing.

He told them the whole story. He admitted that he'd been confused and confessed that for a while he had thought it was all in his imagination, a dream of some sort, or a misunderstanding. Maybe it had been a television program on loud. Maybe it had been nothing.

He told them about cutting his foot on the broken glass and how that made him realize he had really overheard something being planned in the other room. He did not mention the chocolate bar, as he knew that would immediately send Nish's thoughts elsewhere, and he needed all three of his friends to concentrate hard on what he was saying.

The two girls listened intently. Nish half listened, but at least he shut up and let Travis do all the talking.

Sam was the first to say it was the Stanley Cup. She said it so matter-of-factly that Travis instantly knew this was exactly what he himself believed but had been too afraid to say. He'd thought for sure they would tell him he'd been dreaming, that there was no way someone would try to steal the cup again.

"They plan to steal the cup," Sam said again, carefully thinking it through. "They have some inside help with the key to the room where it's being kept. And they have to do it in the morning before the cup is taken over to the Winter Classic."

"I say it's a bank machine they're after," said Nish, trying to look and sound serious at the same time. A difficult task for Nish.

"Too heavy for a duffel bag," said Sarah.

"But it's money!" Nish protested. "What are you going to do with the Stanley Cup? Hide it in your basement and hold it over your head like you won it or something?"

"Ransom, dummy," Sam sneered. "You couldn't find a bank machine with as much money as they'd get for giving the cup back."

"I think Sam's right," said Sarah. "Besides, what would they need to switch a room key for if it was the lobby bank machine they were after? If what you heard is right, Travis, then the plan is to get it away from the hotel as quickly as possible, and without anyone seeing or becoming suspicious. That's why they have the guy pretending to be a hockey player and why they're going to use the Incline. Once he gets up top with the cup in the equipment bag, he can load it into a car and be away without anyone seeing."

"Without surveillance cameras," Nish said. "They have them all around the hotel parking lot."

Travis looked anew at his old friend. "You're sure?" he asked.

Nish nodded knowingly. "I'm sure."

"Nish always likes to know when he's on camera," Sam giggled.

"Har! Har!" Nish sneered.

"Makes sense," said Sarah. "If they loaded it into a car anywhere near the hotel, they'd have it on video. The cameras would pick up the license plate number. But up on top of the hill, there'd be no danger of that."

Travis posed the question that had been troubling him all along.

"How do we stop them?"

16

A plan was in place.
The four Screech Owls – Travis, Sarah, Sam, and Nish – agreed that there was little point in going to anyone with a story about how Travis, groggy from concussion, had overheard two men planning to do something Sunday morning that involved one of the hotel staff. He had never heard them specifically mention the Stanley Cup. He had never seen their faces, so there was no possibility of identifying them from police photos.

Not only would the Owls be dismissed outright, likely even laughed at, but the robbers, if they were indeed robbers, would get away once they realized a security watch had been put on the room where the Stanley Cup was stored.

The Owls' plan was to assign watches: someone to watch the front desk, someone the room, someone the exit to the fire escape. And, if necessary, they needed to get quickly to the Incline up Mount Washington. That was where, if Travis was right, the thieves planned to take the bag containing the cup to a getaway car waiting at the top. Travis was sure he had overheard that, as sure as he could be of anything lately. Whenever he tried to think it all through, he felt dizzy, almost sick. But he said nothing to the others.

They would keep each other informed by texting. Sam had a phone, and Fahd was happy to hand his over to Travis for the morning. Travis hadn't explained what it was for – it would be too embarrassing if nothing happened – and Fahd assumed Travis was calling his parents in Tamarack.

They met early Sunday morning, gathering first in a quiet corner downstairs. The four went over the plan carefully, step by step, each one repeating the plan exactly so it would be memorized.

They rapped their fists together in a pact. Sarah had the last words.

"Let's roll!"

Travis's job was to watch the front desk. He found a seat in the lobby and pretended to be deeply interested in *The Hockey News*. Reading still bothered him, so he just flicked through the magazine and looked at the pictures. He could hear the kitchen staff setting up for the Sunday brunch, and some of the guests were already gathered about the coffee machine talking and refilling their cups.

"*I'm right!*" Travis said to himself when he saw the elevator doors open and the keeper of the Stanley Cup step out. The man looked slightly miffed. He had the key card for his room in his right hand and was impatiently tapping it on the thumb of his left hand.

The keeper of the cup crossed immediately to the reception desk. There was a face behind the desk that Travis hadn't seen before – a man with a white goatee and wire-rimmed glasses. He looked like a kindly doctor, Travis thought. But he knew different.

Travis could not hear what they were saying, but he didn't need to. The keeper of the cup handed over his key, and the white-bearded man, obviously apologizing, took it down to the far end of the long mahogany desk.

Travis moved closer to the desk. The keeper of the Stanley Cup wasn't watching his key being reprogrammed. He was scanning the sports section of *USA Today*. But Travis saw what was happening. The man behind the desk reprogrammed the keeper's key, then slipped a second plastic card into the machine, waited a moment, and removed it. There were now two keys to the room that held the Stanley Cup.

With another apology, the man handed over one of the keys to the keeper of the cup.

"Not to worry," the keeper replied with a smile.

But Travis knew there was plenty to worry about.

He took out Fahd's phone and sent the others a message.

"They have a copy of the key!"

17

S arah was watching the room. Sam walked by
her, relayed what Travis had reported, and kept
walking. Sam would set up watch at the far end of
the hall, where the stairs for the fire escape were.

Sarah stood, flipping through one of the news-
papers stacked on a small table near the elevators.
It wasn't long before one of the elevator doors
opened and the keeper of the cup got off. She
waited until he had turned down the corridor
before following. He tried the key by waving it

near the lock on his door, there was a quick buzz, and he opened the door and stepped in.

If this key worked, then the copy would also work.

Sarah stayed down at the far end of the hall, kneeling, as if she were retying her shoes. Very shortly, the door to the room opened again and the keeper stepped out and headed for the elevators. He was going to brunch downstairs. He would return for the cup later, as the final was scheduled for 1:00 p.m. at Heinz Field and the cup was to be on display for the fans to take photographs. The winning team would then pose with the cup for their championship photo.

Sarah knew this was never going to happen unless the four Owls could stop the thieves from making off with the cup. She walked quickly down the hall to where Sam was waiting, and Sam sent Travis a message.

Travis and Nish were together in the lobby when the message arrived. "Room now empty." They watched as the elevator doors opened and the keeper of the cup stepped out. He went immediately to the dining area, which had just opened for the Sunday brunch.

As the keeper of the cup passed by the two Owls, two men passed them in the other direction. One was short and heavy, the other tall and skinny. They made an odd couple. The tall one had long hair, the short one no hair. The tall one wore all black, the short one a rainbow of colors, a bright-green down jacket, and orange track pants. Pretty dumb, Travis thought, if you want to pass unnoticed.

The two men waited to make sure the keeper was indeed going into brunch, then pushed the elevator button to go up. Travis noticed that the short, stumpy man carried something folded tightly and wrapped in plastic. He knew what it would be: a brand-new hockey equipment bag.

Travis sent a quick text message to the girls: "They're coming."

He and Nish watched as the numbers on the elevator rose, finally stopping at the floor where the girls were keeping watch.

"Let's go!" Travis said.

The boys moved toward the back of the building and pushed through a rear door that overlooked the river and the city on the far side. It was snowing more heavily now, large flakes floating down slowly onto the river and vanishing as they hit the water.

"Over there!" Nish hissed, and poked Travis in the ribs.

Travis turned. Standing to the side of the building was a young man, and he had a hockey stick in his hands.

"Keep going," Travis whispered. They headed around the building in the opposite direction, not even looking back.

They were headed for the Incline.

Sarah and Sam held their breath as they crouched in the stairwell with the door partially opened so that they could see down the corridor. They heard the elevator doors open and close and then saw the two men moving along the hallway.

Sam giggled. Sarah knew why. The tension was one thing, but you couldn't help laugh at the sight of these two strange men.

The short man had a key card out. They stopped in front of the room that held the Stanley Cup and he waved the key in front of the lock. There was a buzz, the lock opened, and the two men quickly entered the room.

"We'd better hightail it," Sarah said. "They might come down by the stairs."

The two girls raced down the hallway, past the room, to the main elevators. They were fairly certain the two men would not come that way, and if they did, the two girls would simply act as if they were guests waiting for the elevator, just like the men.

After several minutes, they heard a door close in the hallway. Sam couldn't resist a look.

It was the men. This time the tall one was carrying a new hockey equipment bag — and it was stuffed with something heavy. They weren't heading for the fire exit; they were coming in Sam and Sarah's direction.

Sam's intake of breath caused Sarah to look. The elevator announced its arrival with a *ping*, and Sarah pulled Sam closer to the doors. They had to follow the plan, even if it meant getting on the same elevator as the thieves.

But the men weren't coming. They stopped at the service elevator. The doors of the service elevator opened, and Sarah caught a glimpse of one of the hotel staff – a man with a white beard and glasses. She hadn't seen him before.

The doors closed on both elevators.

When the girls arrived at the lobby, they got out and moved to the corridor where the service elevator came down, but it had stopped at the second floor.

"They must be getting out there and taking the stairs," Sarah said.

"It's coming again," said Sam.

They heard the elevator stop, and the doors opened. Out stepped the white-bearded man, who headed immediately for the front desk. He seemed nervous, licking the sides of his mustache like a snake.

"C'mon," Sarah said.

18

"**I** can't do it!"

Nish seemed frozen, unable to move.

Travis was frantic. He shook off the rising dizziness once, twice, cleared his head, and acted. "We have to do it!" he shouted at his friend. "*Now get on!*"

The plan was on the verge of falling apart. Travis knew the thieves were on their way. The two Screech Owls were to go up the Incline ahead of the robbers and see if they could get a photo of the getaway car with Fahd's phone. Then, if they could do it, they were to stop the thieves from getting all the way to the top by shutting down the Incline.

The girls would be at the bottom, following the thieves but not trying to stop them. That would be dangerous, and all four of the Owls knew it. If they were going to stop the theft, it would have to be with their brains, not their brawn.

"*You're coming!*" Travis shouted, and with all his might he pushed Nish onto the empty cable car waiting at the bottom of the Incline. He was surprised at his own strength. But he was desperate.

Travis put enough coins into the slot to start the cable pulling them up the side of Mount Washington. The car moved slowly and had windows on all sides, so Travis could see the metal tracks and the cables inching them up the hill. He looked out through the snow at the city below. It looked magical. Peaceful. Completely in contrast with what Travis was experiencing inside. He knew he was still feeling the concussion. He knew he probably shouldn't be there any more than he should be playing. But he couldn't quit. He had to go on. He shook off the sick feeling and steeled himself to do whatever was necessary.

"*I'M GONNA HURL!!!!*"

Nish was crouching on the floor in a corner. It looked like he was praying – and perhaps he was. Travis had almost forgotten Nish's terrible fear of heights. He was scared silly.

"Keep your eyes covered," Travis said. "We're halfway up."

Sarah and Sam crouched at the side of the building, just out of sight of the rear door heading out on the river side. They saw the guy with the hockey stick – "Some *player*," Sam said, "he doesn't even have it taped!" – and watched as the door opened and the tall skinny guy and the short fat guy came out, the short fat guy holding the door open as the tall skinny guy swung the duffel bag out, careful not to hit it on the door frame.

Sam took a quick photograph with her phone.

The handoff took mere seconds. The young guy with the hockey stick put the stick on one shoulder and slung the equipment bag over the other. He seemed fit and strong, and when he began quickly walking away, he did indeed look just like a hockey player heading off to practice or a game of shinny.

The other two thieves went back through the door, which the short man had kept open with a foot. "Good thing you took that shot of them," Sarah said. "We can give it to the police."

Sam nodded. The two girls slipped out of their hiding place and moved quickly across the rear of the hotel, snow now stinging their faces as they ran into the wind.

"We're here!" Travis said.

Nish, red-faced and teary, bolted with a groan of relief out of the cable car and onto the platform overlooking the city. But if Nish felt relief, Travis felt none. Inside his head, everything was in turmoil. He knew where he should be – back in bed, resting in the dark – but here he was: right in the middle of a very, very serious situation. The dizziness faded in and out. Travis knew he had to concentrate.

The two boys walked along to the first look-out and pretended to be taking photographs of the city with Fahd's phone. They could not help but notice the large black SUV parked near the entrance to the Incline. A man was sitting in it, smoking, and he kept checking his watch.

The cable car was headed back down the hill, empty. That meant someone below had called for it.

Travis and Nish walked back while Travis very discreetly managed to take several pictures of the black vehicle, making sure to get the license.

They went to another observation post and pretended to be taking more photographs, then began wandering back toward the Incline.

Travis walked close enough to the edge that he could see the cable car at the bottom.

It was coming up!

It was time for the final piece of the Owls' plan.

While Nish pretended to be paying for more tickets for the Incline, Travis edged his way over to a small cabin-like building where they must have sold tickets in the past. Now it was all done by machine. There was no one there to help them.

Travis knew what he'd find there; he'd seen it earlier when he and Nish arrived at the top. A red button under a sign saying "EMERGENCY STOP."

There was a notice announcing a fine for misuse and warnings not to touch the button unless there was a real emergency.

The stealing of the Stanley Cup qualifies, Travis thought. He looked back down. Sarah and Sam were at the bottom. Sarah had an arm in the air. She could see Travis.

He waited until the cable car was halfway up. Then he pushed the emergency button.

Immediately the Incline rattled to a stop.

"*Keep moving!*" Travis hissed at his friend.

The two boys moved along, heading for another observation platform. Travis hoped it looked as if they'd decided to stay up a while longer rather than head back down.

He knew that, right now, Sam would be calling the police.

He heard a car door slam. He turned and saw that the man in the black suv was now out of the car, checking his watch again and seemingly greatly concerned about something. He began walking toward the Incline.

"Can he start it up again?" Nish asked.

"*I don't know*," Travis replied. He felt a surge of dizziness, thought he was going to throw up.

Before the man could reach the Incline station, however, the boys heard sirens coming along the street at the top of Mount Washington. But it wasn't police sirens. It was the fire department.

A large fire truck, lights flashing, sirens screaming, whipped around the corner, past the two boys, and came to a grinding halt at the Incline.

"Sam called the *fire service*?" Nish asked, astonished.

"It must have been the Emergency Stop button," Travis said. "It automatically calls the nearest fire station the second it's pushed."

Firemen were running into the Incline station. Travis was running now, too. The man who had been waiting up top was hurrying back to his vehicle.

"*Stop!*" Travis found himself yelling at the firemen. "*Call the police! The man trapped in the cable car down there stole the Stanley Cup!*"

But there was no need. Sam had already called the police. Other sirens were now screaming, one cop car pulling up at the bottom of the Incline, where the girls were waiting, two coming fast into the area at the top, where the fire truck was.

The man in the black suv was backing up, his tires squealing.

Nish was running toward the two police cars, his face like a pumped red beach ball.

"*Don't let him out!*" Nish screamed. "*He's the getaway driver!*"

The first policeman out of his car looked at Nish as if he were making some sort of joke, but he held up his hand to stop the black vehicle from leaving. The man opened the door, stepped out, and started running.

Two other police officers gave chase, the three running along the walkway toward the observation deck. They arrived at the same time, the policeman in the lead tackling the driver just as he stepped onto the platform.

Nish turned to Travis, his eyes wide as pucks and blazing.

"Did you see that?" Nish said. "I caught him! I'm the one who got him!"

19

"*Next time*," Billings had warned Travis with a smile.

Travis could not believe that "next time" had come so quickly.

The day had been a whirlwind. The Screech Owls had foiled the theft of the Stanley Cup *for a second time* – only this time it was the presentation cup that the players actually got to hold. The firemen had started the Incline again and brought it to the top of Mount Washington. The man inside the cable car had at first tried to pretend he was nothing more than a pickup hockey player on his way to a game when a couple of foolish kids had pushed the emergency button. But when he saw the police waiting, and when he saw the driver of the suv in handcuffs, he knew the jig was up. He put down his untaped hockey stick, handed over the bulging equipment bag, and raised his hands.

There was much excitement back at the hotel. The keeper of the cup had eaten his brunch and returned to his room. His key still worked fine, but the Stanley Cup was gone. He was calling the police himself when they showed up at the hotel with the cup in the backseat of their cruiser.

Thanks to the photograph taken by Sam of the thieves handing over the cup to the fake hockey player at the back of the hotel, the police were able to round up the two men. They'd been loading their car in the parking lot, just about to leave. And they also took into custody the white-bearded man who had copied the key.

There'd been no time for newspaper and television interviews, to Nish's great disappointment.

There was no time for anything but for the four Owls to join their teammates for a light meal before the shuttle over to Heinz Field and the championship game of the Peewee Winter Classic.

Travis couldn't believe it. The Owls would be meeting the Portland Panthers to decide the championship. The winners would have their photographs taken at center ice with the most famous trophy in the world: the Stanley Cup.

Mr. Dillinger had explained how it all worked out after the round-robin. The Owls were on top in points; the Panthers, who had been beaten by the Owls, were in second place, tied with another team. But as the Portland team had defeated this team in the one match they had played together, the Panthers ranked higher.

The Owls would be playing Billings and Yantha. Travis's old familiar foes – and friends.

Travis was standing by the boards, watching the other Owls go through a team warm-up, when he felt a light tap on the side of his arm. It was Billings, smiling.

Not a word was said between them. The little Portland defenseman skated away quickly, going backward, his stick raised in a quick stick salute for Travis.

"I've never seen so many fans," Sara said, looking up from the bench.

"Me neither," said Travis.

He was excited, but shattered at the same time. He wouldn't be playing. Even though it was the championship game, even though he now felt 100 percent recovered – he'd almost forgotten about his concussion during the plan to thwart the theft of the Stanley Cup – there was no way Muck or Mr. D would allow him to play until he had been cleared by the doctor back home. As Muck put it, "Winning today means nothing if you lose tomorrow." Travis wasn't sure what Muck meant by that, but it sounded good, and he figured it was about the importance of showing caution.

Too bad he wasn't playing, though. Heinz Field was an amazing scene. The snow had stopped, and it was a gorgeous winter afternoon. The ice on the outdoor rink glistened from a fresh flood. The sun danced between scudding clouds.

And the noise! Travis had never heard such noise – even in a covered arena. The stands were packed with thousands of fans and family. The crowd roared like an animal when each player's name was announced and his or her hockey card appeared on the scoreboard. They cheered both teams equally, which made it even better. Both Portland and Tamarack were far away from Pittsburgh, so there was no way the stands could be crammed with supporters of just one side.

Travis shivered. Not from the cold or the light wind but from excitement. No Screech Owl had ever played in front of this many people. Not even half this many people.

Muck sent out his first line for the opening face-off. Sarah at center, Simon on left in Travis's spot, Dmitri on right, Nish and Lars back on defense, Jeremy Weathers in net. Travis burned with envy, desperately wishing he were lining up with them.

Mr. Dillinger called over the players on the ice for a quick huddle. The five skaters and Jeremy came and leaned on the boards while Mr. D gave one of those speeches that he thought were inspirational and the players thought were hilarious. "There has never *been* a larger crowd for a peewee hockey game," he told them. "You have a chance here to make history! The day the great Fred Shero's Philadelphia Flyers won the Stanley Cup, Shero said to the team, 'Win today and we walk together forever!'" The players on the bench slammed their gloves into the boards while the players on the ice cracked their sticks again and again on the ice.

When the sound died down, there was only Sam's voice, cutting through the roar of the huge crowd.

"Hey, Fat Boy – didn't you forget to streak?"

Nish punched his helmet tight to his head and stuck out his tongue at her.

"Tournament's not over yet!"

20

It certainly wasn't over.

Big Yantha won the opening face-off by spinning on his skates so his size blocked Sarah and he had time to kick the puck onto his blade and fire it back to little Billings on defense.

Billings did something unusual then. Instead of mounting an attack, he skated back into his own end, stopping behind his net and softly stickhandling while staring down the ice as if he were calmly looking out over the river.

The crowd roared with impatience. It might have been the roar, might have been Billings's seeming lack of focus, but whatever it was it caused Simon to rush hard at Billings on the forecheck.

This, of course, was exactly what the smart little Portland defenseman wanted. As Simon came drifting around the Panthers' goal, Billings clipped a pass to himself off the bottom bar of the back of the net. Simon went flying by, and when he tried to turn to steal the bouncing puck, he lost an edge and went spilling into the corner.

Billings was already at the blue line when Simon regained his skates. Billings floated a pass up to Yantha, who knocked it down with his glove at the Owls' blue line and, with a quick leap over Lars's stick, was in clean with the puck. A shoulder deke and Jeremy went down, his pads opening just enough for Yantha to slip the puck in the five-hole.

Travis watched the scoreboard flick up the score: 1–0 Panthers. The scoreboard showed a full replay – they had cameras here, covering several angles! – and Travis had to wonder if it would have been different if he'd been on the ice instead of

Simon. He knew Billings's little play off the back of the net. He didn't think he would have been fooled. But who knew for sure? It was unfair to think the goal was Simon's fault. Maybe it was Lars's fault for playing the puck instead of the man. Maybe it was Jeremy's fault for letting his five-hole open up like the Zamboni doors.

Maybe it was no one's fault. Maybe it was all about credit – credit to Billings for making the play, credit to Yantha for finishing it. What was it Muck called it? Yeah, *puck luck*.

The Owls fought back hard through the opening period. But they had trouble breaking through the neutral zone, as the Panthers coach always had a winger dropping back and only rarely did they forecheck.

Travis had a new vantage point to see Muck at work. He'd always been either on the ice or sitting on the bench in front of Muck. And Muck so rarely yelled or said anything at all that Travis realized he hardly knew what his coach did during an actual game. Now Travis was standing behind the players' bench with Mr. Dillinger and Muck – and he was seeing his coach in a whole new way.

Muck hated "trap" hockey. He didn't even like the old saying that good defense was good offense. He liked to say, "Good offense is good offense – period." He liked to call his style of coaching "attack hockey," meaning you always pressed forward. You took care of your own end, you lived up to your defensive responsibilities, but you always looked for the moment to attack and score.

Muck wasn't a numbers guy, and he wasn't much of a chalkboard guy. "You're not building a house," he used to say about coaches who were always diagramming plays in the final minutes of games, "you're playing a game." Muck often said that the most important thing to understand in hockey was that "things happen" out there, and much of play is reflex. You know your position, you know your responsibilities, but you must always be ready to take advantage of the unexpected. It could be a lucky bounce. It could be the puck coming off the glass or boards oddly. It could be an opponent losing an edge or making a mistake. It could be an opposing defenseman joining the rush when he or she should not have joined. You see an opening, Muck would say, you race through it.

The Panthers were doing none of this. Travis could hear the Portland coach telling his players what to do: *"Dump it in!"* *"Stay back!"* *"Stay with your man!"* *"Chip it out!"* *"Don't let them through!"*

It didn't make for a great game to watch, and Travis could sense the restlessness of the fans, who had come out in the open air of winter to cheer for a bunch of twelve-year-old hockey players. They expected more, and, as luck would have it, Nish was about to give it to them.

One of the advantages of having the Panthers play this way – staying back, hardly ever forechecking – was that it gave the Owls' good puck-carrying defensemen, Nish and Lars in particular, but also Sam when she wanted to, plenty of space in which to set up and begin a rush.

And if you handed Wayne Nishikawa opportunities like that, he would seize them.

Travis watched the game slowly turn in the Owls' favor. First Nish and then Lars would come up over the Owls' blue line and hit center with the puck, all the while watching for a break play in which they could send a forward in.

Nish gobbled up the puck in the right corner and skated quickly to the back of the Owls' net. He stood, stickhandling, just as Billings had done on the opening goal, but none of the Panthers fell for it. They stayed back, the closest checker doing figure eights around the Owls' blue line as he waited for Nish to make his move.

Nish came out on the left, stickhandling slowly and looking far up ice. Dmitri knew the look, and Travis saw him dash, quick as a weasel, across center.

Nish had the puck on his backhand, and it seemed he was about to pass over to Lars, but instead of doing as the Panthers expected, Nish launched a high "football" pass that went right over the heads of the two Portland players backing up at center and landed with a slap on the ice right in front of Dmitri.

Dmitri flew in on the right side, and Travis felt like he didn't even have to look. Forehand fake, backhand, puck roofed so hard the goaltender's water bottle spun like a top through the air, spraying water as it slammed into the boards.

Travis looked at Muck, who was leaning in to say something to Mr. Dillinger over the din of the crowd.

"We needed that," Muck shouted. "Now they *have* to play."

Travis knew what Muck meant. The Panthers could no longer play the kind of game their coach had them playing – everything geared to defense, just hoping to hang on long enough to win 1–0. With the game tied and the outcome in doubt, both teams would need to score, which meant that the Panthers would have to unleash their offensive skills.

Travis looked across the ice to the Panthers' bench and swore he saw big Yantha lightly clip Billings on the back of his helmet. Billings nodded, smiling.

How strange, Travis thought. They had just been scored on, and yet they seemed happy. Maybe they needed that goal just as much as the Owls did – a goal that would make everyone play the game the way it was supposed to be played.

Attack hockey.

21

Nish had come to life on the Owls' back end. Beet red in the face, sucking air like a vacuum when he was on the bench, bent over and puffing hard between whistles, Nish was the total hockey player, no longer the buffoon. He was never anything in between, thought Travis. The Owls had either the best player on the ice or the worst, and his name was likely to be Wayne Nishikawa.

Sarah put the Owls ahead 2–1 just before the end of the second period, when she swooped up the ice, slipped around a backpedaling defender, and cranked a slap shot in off the far post. The crowd at Heinz Field erupted with a roar that was almost deafening. Travis had to cover his ears as he watched the replay on the big screen and heard again the roar of appreciation. It was one of Sarah's prettiest goals ever.

Between periods, no one in the dressing room said a word. The Owls were exhausted. Nish's face was completely out of sight as he leaned forward and pushed his face into his shin pads. His hair was soaking wet.

Travis walked around the room touching the shoulder of each one of his teammates. He didn't have anything to say, but he wanted to show he was with them. Lars looked up and smiled and nodded. Nish never moved; his face stayed buried.

A whistle called them out for the third period. Muck went to the door, and instead of opening it, he held it shut tight and turned to face the players, all of them getting to their feet and strapping their helmets back on.

"This game is already a 'classic,'" Muck said. "Enjoy it."

Nothing more. Nothing else was needed.

The Owls stormed out onto the freshly flooded ice with shouts of joy and determination, but their shouts were lost in the roar of the crowd, now fully into this great game in which the Owls had come back so wonderfully.

However, the Panthers weren't finished. Yantha and Billings looked like soldiers heading into battle as they took their positions for the opening face-off: eyes straight ahead, jaws clenched, set.

Midway through the third period, Yantha and his right-winger tore up ice on a two-on-one, Sam the only Owls defender back. Fahd had been caught pinching at the Panthers' blue line, and little Billings had been able to chip the puck out off the boards so that Yantha, in full stride, was able to pick it up.

Sam played the two-on-one perfectly. She knew Yantha would keep – he had the good shot, the winger not so good – and so she stayed between the two forwards until Yantha made his expected fake to send a saucer pass over for the one-timer.

Sam never went for it. She gambled and slid in front of Yantha, who was already into his shot. The wrist shot was hard and accurate, headed for the top corner of Jeremy's net, but Sam had it first and blocked the shot perfectly.

The puck spilled out toward the middle of the ice. Andy Higgins, coming back hard, reached to take it.

But he never found it.

Little Billings had been coming up just as hard to join the rush, and he was able to lift Andy's stick from behind so that Andy, turning sharply to go back the other direction, found himself leaving the Owls' end without the puck. Billings now had the puck on his stick.

Billings faked a pass to the other winger, then fed to Yantha, who drilled a shot high on Jeremy's blocker side and into the net.

Tie game.

The Winter Classic was going to overtime. After Yantha's pretty goal tied it – Andy punching himself on the bench as he watched the replay – the two teams both had chances, but no one could put the puck in.

There would be no flood. They would play five minutes overtime, four-on-four. And if there was no result, they would go to a shootout. Whichever team was ahead after five shooters would win. If tied after five, they would shoot until one team held the lead.

Muck sent out Sarah, Dmitri, Nish, and Lars to take the first shift. Travis ached to be with them. He looked down the bench and saw little Simon Milliken and realized Simon was aching just as badly to be out there.

There seemed twice as much ice with four skaters a side rather than five. Sarah and Dmitri, with their fabulous skating, were all over the ice, but they couldn't break through the Panthers' defense.

Nish had one good rush and cranked a shot off the crossbar that went up over the glass and so far out of play it almost landed in the football stands. They replayed the shot on the scoreboard, and the cameras followed the puck right to its final resting place, the crowd roaring and cheering with delight.

Travis looked at Nish as Nish watched the replay, the big defenseman's tomato face twisting in agony as he saw how close he had come to winning the championship.

Yantha had an equally good chance for the Panthers, getting off a quick one-timer that Jeremy somehow snagged just as it was heading into the top corner. When they replayed the save on the scoreboard, Jeremy received a standing ovation – and from what Travis saw in the replay, it was well deserved. It was a spectacular save.

The horn went all too soon. No one had scored. They would go to a shootout.

Muck hated shootouts. It wasn't team play, he said, and it wasn't hockey. "May as well decide by throwing horseshoes," he liked to say. "Or darts."

But the Screech Owls loved them. They loved to practice them at the end of workouts. They loved to watch them on the NHL highlights. They liked to try trick shots like spinneramas or between-the-skates or even picking the puck up off the ice and trying to throw it, lacrosse-style, into the net.

Muck and Mr. Dillinger filled out the card for the shootout. Travis was close enough to see the names being scribbled down.

1. Sarah Cuthbertson
2. Dmitri Yakushev
3. Lars Johanssen
4. Samantha Bennett
5. Wayne Nishikawa

Travis wondered if he'd have been on the list if he'd been playing. Of course he would, he told himself. He would have replaced Sam, perhaps even Lars. The other three were a given. That Muck wanted Nish last showed that, despite all Muck's mutterings about the ridiculous Iceman, he still had faith in Nish's ability to come through when everything was on the line.

The referee called for a coin toss, and the Panthers won the right to choose first or second. Their coach chose first. Muck would have done the same. If you could score that first goal, you might panic the other side.

Yantha, to no one's surprise, was tapped to go first for Portland. He was the one most likely to score, and his goal would put pressure on the Owls.

Yantha came down the ice fast, then stopped hard in a spray of snow as Jeremy went down. Yantha used his long reach to sweep the puck around Jeremy and into the net.

The Panthers were 1–0 in the shootout.

Jeremy pounded his stick on the ice and took a shot of water as they replayed the goal on the scoreboard. Travis saw Muck shaking his head. These weren't real goals in Muck's opinion; they were trick goals, with no place in the game of hockey. The trickier the better, thought the Owls. Travis wondered if he would have had the guts to try the Finnish-lacrosse shot if he'd been playing. Not likely, he thought – too embarrassing if he missed.

Sarah went in as if it were a real game, skating fast and deking. She made a good move, but the Panthers' goaltender covered up his five-hole, and Sarah's low slider failed to find the back of the net.

The Panthers shot, and missed.

Dmitri clanged his backhand off the crossbar.

The Panthers shot a third time, and Jeremy, spinning like a crocodile in his crease, just caught the puck with his arm as it was about to cross the line.

Lars shot, and the Panthers' goalie made a fine blocker save.

The Panthers took a fourth shot and failed to beat Jeremy, who held his ground.

It was Sam's turn. She was red-faced, and if Travis hadn't known better, he'd have said she was crying. This was an unusual position for Sam to be in. She was more a defensive player than offensive, but she was still good on the attack. Normally, this would have been Travis's shot, and she likely knew it. The pressure was enormous.

Sam skated slowly with the puck – too slowly, Travis thought – and came in on a wide sweep that curled from one face-off dot to the other while passing in front of the Portland net.

Travis cringed. It was a mistake, he thought. All the Portland goaltender had to do was stay with Sam, keep low, and she would have nothing to shoot at.

But then Sam did the strangest thing. She let the puck leave the blade of her stick and she skated right by it. The puck just sat there while the goalie followed Sam, anticipating a backhand attempt. Sam then swirled around and lunged at the puck she had left behind her, falling to the ice as her stick swept the puck into the net.

The Portland coach went nuts, screaming at the referees and jumping right up onto the boards. He was furious. He said the goal didn't count, because the forward motion had been stopped. The rule was clear – you had to keep the puck going toward the net.

The officials said they would check on the replay, and the play went up on the scoreboard. They slowed the play down so much it seemed to creep by.

When the crowd saw that, indeed, the puck had still been going forward, even if at a snail's pace, they cheered their approval.

The referee blew his whistle and pointed to center ice.

Good goal. Shootout tied.

It was Billings's turn to shoot. He seemed remarkably relaxed, Travis thought. Billings stood at his own blue line, staring down the ice, and waited for the referee's signal to go.

Billings picked up the puck at center and came in straight at Jeremy. He faked shot, faked backhand, went back to forehand as Jeremy went down, and the puck skipped off Jeremy's chest protector and into the air, spinning and wobbling.

It seemed even slower than Sam's goal, Travis thought – and this wasn't even slow motion.

He watched, helpless, as the puck landed on Jeremy's shoulder, trickled down onto the ice, and slipped over the line just as Jeremy's stick arrived to stop it.

The crowd roared its appreciation and roared again as the replay appeared on the clock.

It was all up to Nish.

If Nish scored, the shootout would continue. If he failed, the Owls were out.

Travis looked at his friend. Nish's back was hunched over, his stick across his knees, head straight down as he waited for the crowd to settle down and the puck to be returned to center.

"*Do it, Fat Boy!*" Sam shouted from the bench.

"*You the man!*" Jesse Highboy shouted.

Nish paid them no heed. He was all business.

The referee signaled it was time. Nish straightened up and headed for the puck, picking it up easily despite the fallen snow, and he began moving in on the Portland net.

Nish seemed to be deciding what to do. He stickhandled a few times, then picked up speed, coming in hard. Instead of faking, he ripped a shot from out beyond the slot, catching everyone off guard, including the Portland goaltender.

Nish's shot flew past the Panthers' goalie's shoulder – and clanged hard off the crossbar.

Up over the net the puck flew. Up over the glass. Up over the field – almost to the stands.

The entire field groaned, and groaned again when they saw it on the replay.

And then the crowd began cheering. Slowly at first, then building to a tremendous roar, every one of the thousands of fans on their feet and cheering.

The Portland Panthers had won the Peewee Winter Classic.

The Zamboni doors opened, and the keeper of the cup, dressed in a fine suit and wearing white gloves, came onto the ice carrying the Stanley Cup.

The crowd cheered louder for this than they had for any of the goals. The Stanley Cup was the hero of this game, not any of the youngsters who had played it.

First, though, the teams shook hands. Muck and Mr. Dillinger led the way, Muck very generously congratulating the Portland coach on his team's win. Travis hurried to join in the line, for the first time ever shaking hands with opponents when he was in a tracksuit and boots rather than hockey equipment and skates.

The last player in the Portland line was Billings, the player who had scored the shootout goal that won the championship.

Billings looked at Travis and smiled a huge smile.

"Next time," Billings said.

"Next time," Travis said, trying to smile, too.

But he felt like crying.

22

Nish was despondent.

"I'm worried about him," Sarah said to Travis. "He won't speak to anyone. He won't listen. He acts as if he'd like to throw himself in the river out there."

Travis shuddered at the thought. But nothing anyone could say – not even Sam, who always had a way of getting to him – could bring Nish out of his funk. Twice he'd had the championship on his stick, and twice he'd skipped his shot off the cross-bar and into the football field.

The Owls were back at the hotel. Burning with envy, they had watched the Portland Panthers taking turns hoisting the world's most famous sports trophy over their heads and skating about the Heinz Field arena while the huge crowd stayed on its feet and cheered. Each player was shown close up on the scoreboard as he or she received the Stanley Cup. Many were openly crying.

Some of the Owls were crying, too, but not for joy. Travis had seen Sarah wipe away tears; Jeremy, too, who thought he should have had the Billings goal; and Simon, who felt he had let the line down. They were all wiping their eyes. But no one was to blame. It just happened. The Panthers deserved their victory this day, just as the Owls had deserved their earlier victory over them.

Nish took it harder than anyone. He, too, had been crying. Travis saw no tears when he finally spoke to his friend, but Nish's eyes were so red it looked like they'd been dragged through a rosebush.

"Not your fault," Travis said.

"Bug off," Nish answered.

"No one's fault," Travis said.

"Drop dead."

Mr. Dillinger had ordered pizza, and they were gathered in the ballroom of the hotel. There was a huge bowl filled with ice and drinks of every kind – Gatorade, pop, juice – and some of the Owls were lining up to eat.

Travis left Nish to his thoughts and found Sarah across the room, staring out over the water. "I'm worried about Nish," he told her.

"Everybody's blaming themselves," said Sarah. "We're all hurting. But I've never seen Nish like this. We'd better keep an eye on him. He's not himself."

Travis nodded. He'd keep a careful eye on his friend. He looked back to where he'd left Nish, but Nish was no longer there. There was a washroom just around the corner; he'd likely gone there to cry some more, out of sight of anyone who might tease him. Travis felt terrible for his friend. It hadn't been Nish's fault. It was nobody's fault.

As Travis looked around the room, he noticed

something at the doorway. Muck was there, holding the door open.

And in walked the Stanley Cup.

Well, actually, it was carried in by the keeper of the cup. He still had his suit and white gloves on. He was smiling. The Owls, roaring their approval, raced over.

"You kids deserve this," the keeper said. "The Pittsburgh police told me all about what happened this morning. If not for you, we wouldn't have been able to have that ceremony at Heinz Field with the Panthers. A couple of the players on the Panthers asked me if I wouldn't mind bringing this over to the hotel so you could have your pictures taken with it – how's that for sportsmanship?"

Travis didn't have to ask who. He knew. Billings and Yantha.

Travis felt the blood rise in his face, but this time there was no dizziness. Just happiness. Pure happiness.

"So, in appreciation of the Screech Owls saving the Stanley Cup at the Winter Classic," the keeper said, "the Hockey Hall of Fame would like to allow each of you to have your picture taken holding the cup."

"Up?" asked Fahd.

The keeper stared at him, not following.

"Like, over our heads?" Fahd repeated.

"Of course," the keeper said, smiling.

"But I thought only winners were allowed to do that," Fahd persisted.

"You *are* winners," the keeper said. "Every single one of you. But especially the four Owls who set the trap for those thieves. Where are you four?"

Sheepishly, Travis, Sarah, and Sam stepped forward with their hands up. Travis knew he was blushing. His face burned.

"Where's the fourth? The big kid?" the keeper asked, looking around.

Travis also looked around. Nish was still nowhere to be seen. How badly was he taking this loss, anyway?

Suddenly, the doors to the ballroom burst open, and in flew a strange apparition that seemed to stun the keeper of the cup.

It was a heavy little peewee hockey player, wearing nothing but a goalie mask, a bed sheet with a huge black line down the middle . . . and his underwear.

"*The Iceman!*" the apparition screamed, then bolted across the room, once around the Stanley Cup, and flew out through the far doors.

Sarah turned to Travis, her face dancing with delight.

"He's back!"

FACE-OFF
AT THE ALAMO

The Screech Owls are deep in the heart of Texas, in the southern city of San Antonio. The town is a surprising hotbed of American ice hockey, and the Owls are excited to come and play in the big San Antonio Peewee Invitational. Between games, they can explore the fascinating canals that twist and turn through the city's historic downtown.

The tournament has been set up to include guided tours of the Alamo, the world's most famous fort, where Davy Crockett fought and died. The championship-winning team will even get to spend a night in the historic fort.

The Screech Owls discover that the Alamo is America's greatest symbol of courage and freedom, and when Travis and his friends uncover a secret plot to destroy it, they must summon all the courage of the fort's original defenders.

MYSTERY AT LAKE PLACID

Travis Lindsay, his best friend, Nish, and all their pals on the Screech Owls hockey team are on their way to New York for an international peewee tournament. As the team makes its way to Lake Placid, excitement builds with the prospect of playing on an Olympic rink, in a huge arena, scouts in the stands!

But as soon as they arrive, things start to go wrong. Their star center, Sarah, plays badly. Travis gets knocked down in the street. And someone starts tampering with the equipment. Who is trying to sabotage the Screech Owls? And can Travis and the others stop the destruction before the final game?

THE NIGHT THEY STOLE THE STANLEY CUP

Someone is out to steal the Stanley Cup – and only the Screech Owls stand between the thieves and their prize!

Travis, Nish, and the rest of the Screech Owls have come to Toronto for the biggest hockey tournament of their lives – only to find themselves in the biggest *mess* of their lives. First, Nish sprains his ankle falling down the stairs at the CN Tower. Later, key members of the team get caught shoplifting. And during a tour of the Hockey Hall of Fame, Travis overhears two men plotting to snatch the priceless Stanley Cup and hold it for ransom!

Can the Screech Owls do anything to save the most revered trophy in the country? And can they rise to the challenge on the ice and play their best hockey ever?

THE GHOST OF THE STANLEY CUP

The Screech Owls have come to Ottawa to play in the Little Stanley Cup Peewee Tournament. This relaxed summer event honors Lord Stanley himself – the man who donated the Stanley Cup to hockey – and gives young players a chance to see the wonders of Canada's capital city, travel into the wilds of Algonquin Park, and even go river rafting.

Their manager, Mr. Dillinger, is also taking them to visit some of the region's famous ghosts: the ghost of a dead prime minister; the ghost of a man hanged for murder; the ghost of the famous painter Tom Thomson. At first the Owls think this is Mr. Dillinger's best idea ever, until Travis and his friends begin to suspect that one of these ghosts could be real.

Who is this phantom? Why has he come to haunt the Screech Owls? And what is his connection to the mysterious young stranger who offers to coach the team?

SUDDEN DEATH IN NEW YORK CITY

Nish has done some crazy things – but nothing to match this! At midnight on New Year's Eve, he plans to "moon" the entire world.

The Screech Owls are in New York City for the Big Apple International Peewee Tournament. Not only will they play hockey in Madison Square Garden, home of the New York Rangers, but on New Year's Eve they'll be going to Times Square for the live broadcast of the countdown to midnight. It will be shown on a giant TV screen and beamed around the world by a satellite. Data and Fahd soon discover that, with just a laptop and video camera, they can interrupt the broadcast – and Nish will be able to pull off the most outrageous stunt ever.

Just hours before midnight, the Screech Owls learn that terrorists plan to disrupt the New Year's celebration. What will Nish do now? And what will happen at the biggest party in history?

SCREECH OWLS

PERIL AT THE WORLD'S BIGGEST HOCKEY TOURNAMENT

The Screech Owls have convinced their coach, Muck, to let them play in the Bell Capital Cup in Ottawa, even though it means spending New Year's away from their families. It's a chance to skate on the same ice rink where Wayne Gretzky played his last game in Canada, and where NHLers like Daniel Alfredsson, Sidney Crosby, and Mario Lemieux have played.

During the tournament, political leaders from around the world are meeting in Ottawa. To pay tribute to the young hockey players, the prime minister has invited the leaders to watch the final game on New Year's Day. The Owls can barely contain their excitement!

Meanwhile, as Nish is nursing an injured knee off-ice, he may have finally found a way to get into the *Guinness World Records*. But what no one knows is that a diabolical terrorist also has plans to make it a memorable – and deadly – game.

ROY MACGREGOR was named a media inductee to the Hockey Hall of Fame in 2012, when he was given the Elmer Ferguson Award for excellence in hockey journalism. He has been involved in hockey all his life, from playing all-star hockey in Huntsville, Ontario, against the likes of Bobby Orr from nearby Parry Sound, to coaching, and he is still playing old-timers hockey in Ottawa, where he lives with his wife Ellen. They have four grown children.

Roy is the author of several classics in hockey literature. *Home Team: Fathers, Sons and Hockey* was shortlisted for the Governor General's Award for Literature. *Home Game* (written with Ken Dryden) was a bestseller, as were *Road Games: A Year in the Life of the NHL*, *The Seven A.M. Practice*, and his latest, *Wayne Gretzky's Ghost: And Other Tales from a Lifetime in Hockey*. He wrote *Mystery at Lake Placid*, the first book in the bestselling, internationally successful Screech Owls series in 1995. In 2005, Roy was named an Officer of the Order of Canada.